COLLISION COURSE
WITH LOVE

Widowed for over a year, Gabby Balfour decides it's time she moved on. She emigrates to Australia intent on new beginnings, but feels guilty that she's alive while her husband's not. When she meets gorgeous entre-preneur Sam Donovan the attraction is instant, yet she's scared to fall in love again, of being vulnerable and open to the pain of loss. But Sam helps her find closure on her grief and guilt, and the courage to embrace a new love.

Books by Sarah Evans
in the Linford Romance Library:

SARAH EVANS

COLLISION COURSE WITH LOVE

Complete and Unabridged

LINFORD
Leicester

First published in Great Britain in 2007

First Linford Edition
published 2010

British Library CIP Data

Evans, Sarah.
   Collision course with love. - -
   (Linford romance library)
   1. Widows- -Fiction. 2. Women immigrants- -
   Australia- -Fiction. 3. Love stories.
   4. Large type books.
   I. Title II. Series
   823.9'2–dc22

   ISBN 978–1–44480–148–4

Published by
F. A. Thorpe (Publishing)
Anstey, Leicestershire

Set by Words & Graphics Ltd.
Anstey, Leicestershire
Printed and bound in Great Britain by
T. J. International Ltd., Padstow, Cornwall

This book is printed on acid-free paper

1

The buzz of the newsroom acted like a swift, strong tonic. Gabby hadn't realised until this moment just how much she had missed working in the hustling, bustling media world. It was as if she had woken from the deepest of sleeps into a brand new dawn jewelled with the dew of hope and fresh beginnings.

The past two years of sorrow and pain were pushed unceremoniously to the background, where, Gabby ruefully acknowledged, they should have been well and truly buried for the last few months.

Those sad memories now blurred and faded as Gabby absorbed the office atmosphere like a dry sponge tossed into water. Just the noise of muted telephones, low, murmuring voices, the odd outbreak of laughter, and the frisson of excitement in the air made her heartbeat kick up its rhythm and hold a faster pace.

She had been so right to come. She could almost feel a heavy, physical weight lift from her chest and float away. For a split second, the illusion made her dangerously light headed.

'Mrs Balfour?'

Gabby swung around. A tall woman with short grey hair and wearing a severely tailored suit was smiling at her inquiringly.

'Yes. That's me,' said Gabby as she struggled to get her newly-released buoyancy under control. She must appear cool and efficient if she wanted to make a good impression.

'This way, please,' said the secretary.

They walked along grey-blue corridors of glass where people worked in small, compact cubicles with computers, until they came to a closed door. The woman knocked and then immediately opened the door. She announced Gabby's name and ushered the young woman into the room.

'He won't eat you,' she said with a twinkle in her eye as Gabby hesitated ever so slightly on the threshold. 'He's already had lunch.'

'I'm so glad.' Gabby smiled back and then gave her full attention to the small, rotund editor who was scrutinising her over the top of his gold-rimmed bifocals.

He resembled a gnome in a business shirt, though without the red pointy hat. He looked sixty-five but was probably younger and had that rumpled, seedy appearance of someone who'd spent too long sitting behind a desk. And the woman had been right about lunch.

Breadcrumbs were liberally sprinkled over his striped-blue shirtfront and on the piles of papers littering his desk.

'Dan Commeri,' he said in way of introduction. His voice was hard with a twang that Gabby was quickly becoming accustomed to hearing in the couple of days she had been in Australia. He didn't rise to shake her hand but instead rocked back in his chair, dusted off some crumbs and then folded his arms over his chest.

'So you want a job.' It was a statement, not a question.

'Yes, that's why I'm here.'

'Sit down. Is that your cuttings file? I'd like to see it.'

Gabby passed the bulky file to him and he silently flicked through the pages, occasionally reading one of the news stories Gabby had written while working on daily and evening papers in England. His gnomish face gave nothing away.

Gabby clenched her hands together and tried to keep her breathing calm and regular. She needed a job. It was a lifeline to her sanity. Since her husband, Mark, had died she had lost her way, her confidence and self-esteem slipping through the open wounds of her grief. If she had any chance of rebuilding her life, it was here, in Perth, where she knew nobody and so could start afresh with no demands or expectations being placed upon her by well meaning family and friends.

'How long have you been a journalist?' said Dan Commeri, pursing his lips over one of her headline articles.

'Eight years. Here are my references from previous employers.' Gabby passed him three business envelopes.

'Why haven't you worked for the past two years?' he asked after reading them.

'My husband contracted leukaemia. I gave up my job to nurse him.'

'Did he get better?'

Gabby's throat convulsively constricted as it always did when telling people about Mark's death for the first time. 'No, he died,' she managed to say after a moment's hesitation. She was glad her voice didn't tremble too much but the editor shot her a short, sharp glance anyway.

'Is that why you've come to Australia?' he said. 'To make a new start?'

'Yes. My husband and I had talked about holidaying here. We'd even discussed emigrating. But we'd never got around to doing anything about it and then he got sick. When Mark died, I decided I should come anyway.'

It had been a sort of therapy. A way to try and grasp the remnants of a precious dream before it completely disappeared into the ether.

And Mark had wanted her to come.

Before he'd got too sick to communicate, he had urged her to make the trip. She had promised, but a part of her was wracked with guilt that she was able to follow their dream while he couldn't.

She also felt cheated and angry that Mark had been taken away from her. It was so unfair that their life together had been cruelly ended before it had had a chance to begin. They'd still had so much living to do.

Deep down she felt even guiltier that she still craved adventure in spite of it all. It felt wrong and disloyal even though Gabby knew that Mark would have understood.

He'd always teased her about her zest for life and had endlessly encouraged her exuberance. He'd been her rock, the foundation that had given her the confidence to fly and try all that she wanted to do. It had been his special, generous gift.

But now he was gone and she had to discover the art of flying solo. It was scary stuff. She was terrified of opening her arms and launching into life, hoping to catch the strong thermals to spiral her high, and then missing them and falling hard.

She was nervous without his steady, grounded presence. Frightened that without him she would fail.

Apart from coping with the terrible sadness and emptiness of Mark's death, this was the next biggest test of her life: to learn to live without him.

Half-an-hour later, all Gabby's doubts had evaporated.

She was euphoric. As she left the editor's office, she was all but bouncing and clicking her heels in the air. She had done it! She had landed a job! OK, so it was only a part-time one, but it was a start. It was a small but significant step in the right direction.

Excitement bubbled deep inside her until she felt she would burst, but there was nobody to tell, nobody with whom she could share her good news. She didn't know a single soul in the city.

But she refused to feel sad about it. She would buy a bottle of wine and celebrate on her own. She deserved it.

Gabby pushed through the big glass doors of The Western Standard's building and stepped straight into the furnace heat of summer. The harsh white glare of the sun momentarily blinded her, but she welcomed it on her skin that was chilled from the air-conditioning and she raised her face towards the sun's warmth, like a flower seeking the light after darkness. She slowly breathed in the scorched air, filling her lungs with its fiery dry heat.

The next moment all the breath was knocked from her body as she collided on her too-high heels but was stopped from falling by strong lean fingers. They wrapped around her arm with a vice-like grip that made her wince.

Still dazzled by the sunlight, Gabby could only make out a silhouette of a tall man towering above her.

'Sorry,' she stammered, blinking rapidly to clear her vision. It didn't help. Her eyes couldn't adjust to the hard, brilliant light that quickly.

'No worries,' said the man. His voice was pure gravel. It shivered across her emotions like sandpaper over skin and Gabby did just that, she shivered.

'You OK?' he rasped, concern under-lying that gorgeous gravel, and Gabby couldn't help but shiver again. His voice was mesmerising. What did he do to make it so delicious? Smoke a thousand cigarettes a day or gargle with blue metal? Perhaps both! Whatever, it was as sexy as hell!

Sexy as hell? Yikes! What was wrong with her? Out of nowhere she was suddenly getting bizarrely personal thoughts about a completely strange man.

It must be because of jetlag.

And securing a job after a two-year drought.

And not eating breakfast . . .

The man was still holding on to her arm and heat that had nothing to do with the hot sun, steamed through her body. She was mortified. She quickly tried to shake off his hand and put distance between them.

But hadn't he just asked her a question? Oh yes. Was she OK? Yes. No. This was ridiculous! Get a grip, girl!

'I'm fine,' she managed to squeak. No low, sexy voice for her. More startled rabbit caught in a snare. She sucked in a desperate breath and tried to calm down.

'You don't feel faint?'

'No.'

'You look very pale. There's a sickbay in the building. Let me take you there to see the nurse before you keel over. She'll make you feel much better.'

'There's nothing wrong with me!' Except for a sudden attack of mushy brain and spaghetti legs. 'No, I'm OK, really,' she stammered. 'I'm only pale because I've come straight out of an English winter. I left snow and ice. I haven't had time to gain a tan yet. But I will. As soon as I've found out where the beach is.'

Which Gabby knew was a stupid thing to say because the city was built on the coast! But she couldn't stop herself from babbling on like an idiot.

'Take my advice, with your fair skin stay out of the sun or it'll burn to rawhide. And wear sunglasses to protect those beautiful baby blues of yours.'

Gabby gaped. Beautiful baby blues? Good grief. Was he trying to pick her up? Well, he mustn't. She wasn't in the market for pick-ups.

Maybe she was giving out all the wrong vibes, flapping about in the Australian sun like a headless chicken? She must get her act together and start playing it cool. She didn't want to be considered a flirt. She'd only been widowed a few months . . .

11

OK, so it had been a year. And the year before that Mark had been so terribly sick and dosed up on pain-killers. So in reality, she'd really been on her own for two years. But did that mean she was ready for the singles game again.

But he was still holding her arm. Gabby tried again to shake off his large tanned hand. Her vision was beginning to adjust now and she found herself gazing into cool grey eyes that were the exact colour of Welsh slate. Well, why wasn't she surprised? They had to be rock-coloured with his voice full of grit and gravel.

And then there was his face. It was so starkly planed it could have been chiselled out of granite by a master sculptor. His cheekbones were high, his jaw square and his nose aquiline with a bump that hinted of an old breakage. The flaw only emphasised his otherwise physical perfection.

His hair was jet-black and slicked back from his brow as if he'd just got out the shower. Flecks of grey winged it at his temples and gave him an air of authority. Not that he needed it. His sheer size and business-suited presence was enough to command one's attention.

And he certainly had Gabby's attention. She had to admit that he was a devastatingly attractive man.

And then she realised with a start that she was staring like some star-struck kid. She blinked and shook her head and then flicked a nervous glance back at the man. There was a definite gleam of humour in his slate-grey eyes and Gabby had the strong impression that he was laughing at her.

'I'll bear it in mind, thank you,' she said as off-balanced as she had been when they'd first collided. 'Now if you're quite finished, I'd like you to let go of my arm.' She stared at it pointedly.

Sam Donovan chuckled. He liked her. She was cute with her auburn hair bobbed and curled at her delicate jaw line and those amazing hyacinth blue eyes wide and suspicious. He hadn't been joking about her skin. It was as fair as whipped cream and would need to be protected from the ravages of the harsh Australian summer sun.

'I wish I had more time. I could show you around the place,' he murmured provocatively and watched the blush creep into those smooth pale cheeks. 'But I'm already late for a meeting so I'll have to say goodbye. Perhaps some other time, Ms . . . ?'

'Goodbye,' she said dismissively, not giving her name. He was acutely aware of the frost in her tone.

'Try not to fall over again,' he said with a wry smile and brushed her cheek before pushing his way through the swing doors of the newspaper building and heading for his office.

* * *

As he rode the lift to the top floor, Sam Donovan mused about the petite auburn-haired beauty. Who was she? He wished he'd had the time to find out but it was imperative he made the meeting. There was a lawsuit against the paper and he had to do some fast-talking with the company lawyers and those of the development tycoon who was trying to sue.

It was all part of the cut and thrust of newspaper life and Sam loved it. But sometimes it would be nice to slow down a little and enjoy the fruits of his hard work and long hours of labour he put in twenty-four-seven.

What was the point in being one of Perth's most wealthy men if you couldn't take time out to enjoy the more pleasant aspects of life?

Such as getting to know that stunning girl . . .

Perhaps it was time he made some important changes to his lifestyle.

2

Gabby took a taxi back to her hotel room and flung her cuttings file and bag on to the couch. She felt in a complete turmoil since colliding with that man outside of Newspaper House. Her stomach was queasy and her head ached.

Perhaps it was because her body was all messed up with the time differences. She'd never experienced jetlag before and she'd heard that it affected people differently.

But did it make some of them susceptible to tall, dark strangers? How cliché!

Gabby kicked off her shoes, poured herself a glass of iced water and flopped herself on to the bed. She was too hot to think. The day had taken its toll. She hoped it wouldn't be too long before she became accustomed to the heat.

Minus temperatures in England hadn't prepared her at all for the one-hundred-degree summer heat of Perth.

She wriggled her toes and let the air conditioning cool her flushed skin.

The cooler she got, the more her brain began to function. But instead of being sensible and contemplating what needed to be done before she began her new appointment the following week — such as a brand new wardrobe with clothes more suited to the incredible heat and somewhere cheaper to live than this fancy hotel — she could only think of Him.

The Man.

The sexy man who had literally floored her.

Gabby groaned and grabbed her pillow, tugging it over her head in a bid to knock out the image of his starkly handsome face and trying vainly to conjure up the familiar features of her late husband.

Really, jetlag was the pits. She wouldn't be in this state if she'd had a decent sleep the night before. Maybe she was being a bit premature starting work so soon after arriving in Australia. But what was the alternative? More empty days and even emptier nights dwelling on the what might have beens?

No, she had been right. It was time to move on. Grab hold of life with two hands and not let it seep through her fingers.

At least she hoped she was right.

She turned her head and looked towards the dressing table. On it was a gilt-framed photograph. She'd placed it there the night she'd arrived, when she'd been unpacking her luggage. It was of Mark.

She'd taken the photo on their first date together when they'd visited Brighton Pier. The bracing salt wind had whipped up the colour in his cheeks and tousled his sandy hair. His green-grey eyes, the colour of that particular day's turbulent sea, were scrunched against the elements. A broad grin was plastered wide on his freckled face.

Gabby's throat clogged tight. How she missed him. How she missed his easy-going nature, his crazy jokes and ability to laugh at the world.

Would she ever get rid of this feeling of emptiness? Would she ever be ready and able to move on and find love and happiness with someone else?

She had to admit that possibility seemed a long way off and not one she could contemplate any time too soon.

'So, Mark,' she said softly. 'Am I doing the right thing? Do you reckon I can cope with this new country and new job?'

She lay still, listening hard to the humming silence, hoping for an answer. It was something she'd slipped into doing when Mark had been so sick in hospital and couldn't speak. And she'd carried on doing it in those first grief-stricken weeks, seeking comfort from the memories of their shared silences.

She supposed it had become a habit. But as it still gave her comfort she wasn't going to give it up in a hurry, however crazy it appeared from the outside.

'And I'm sorry for being such an idiot about That Man,' she confessed. 'Blame the jetlag. I do. Utterly.'

Some time during the hot summer afternoon, Gabby fell into an exhausted sleep. She awoke around one in the morning with her brain pedalling too fast for her to stay in bed.

She got up, showered, raided the bar fridge for snacks and then tried to read. The words jumbled in front of her eyes and made it impossible for her to follow the plot, so she rang home to tell them the good news about her job and then tried to sleep again.

But that was impossible too. A pair of dark eyes prevented even a doze and she remained awake until it was time for breakfast. By then her eyes were all hot and gritty and barely able to stay open so that all she wanted to do was crawl back under the covers and sleep for a week.

The following Monday, Gabby was back at Newspaper House and just about ready to tackle the world and whatever it had in store for her. She felt pretty good and was eager to face any challenges. She'd dressed for the part, wearing one of her new summer outfits. It was a simple crisp, linen shift in a red-russet and made her feel a million dollars.

But it wasn't quite enough to counteract the butterflies of apprehension in her stomach. As soon as she'd arrived at Newspaper House, they had swamped her previous excitement, making her wonder anew if she'd made the right decision.

It was such a big step living and working in another country so far away from all that was familiar and safe.

Mark would have laughed at her doubts and urged her onwards. She took courage from that thought and held on to it tight. She raised a smile, straightened her shoulders and marched through the building's double doors ready to embark on this new phase of her life.

After a detailed briefing from the news-desk editor, Gabby was soon sitting in front of a computer terminal and comfortably working on her first piece. It was a lightweight rewrite of a medical press release and took little time to do. It was a great way to ease herself into the swim.

After she'd filed the story, she was asked by one of her colleagues if she'd like to go to the canteen for a coffee. The girl introduced herself as Sally Essex, one of the senior reporters. She was tall, tanned and blonde and wouldn't have looked out of place on a golden beach in a tiny bikini with a surfboard under her arm.

Sally was warm and friendly and full of information. She talked non-stop as she led Gabby towards the elevators, filling her in on anything and everything that was going on at Newspaper House.

In particular, she explained how entrepreneur, Sam Donovan, had bought the former family-owned newspaper and was giving it a good shake up. 'It was needed, that's for sure. He's injecting zest into the paper. It's a very exciting time for us.'

She gave Gabby an assessing look. 'So you must be something special to be put on staff,' she said. 'Since being taken over by Donovan's Media Entertainment Enterprises, we haven't had any new appointments.'

'It must have been my lucky day,' said Gabby as they waited for the lift. Her mind involuntarily whisked back to that day. She wished it hadn't because suddenly, without a by-your-leave, the image of That Man suddenly swam before her eyes.

Would that he would leave her alone. He'd been plaguing her all week.

When she'd searched for accommodation, she had wondered if he lived nearby and then admonished herself for being such an idiot to think of such a thing.

At night, much to her consternation, he'd also raided her dreams — in full, glorious Technicolour — and she would start awake with a fine sheen of perspiration dampening her skin, her body feeling uneasily restless and unfulfilled.

She seemed to spend all her waking moments trying to wipe him from her mind while apologising to Mark for her disloyalty.

It wasn't fair. The man was a stranger. She hadn't asked for him to invade her life. He should just butt out. Mark was enough for her.

Nevertheless, That Man plagued her. Even now his gorgeous image swam into the forefront of her mind. She blinked to clear the vivid picture.

As she re-opened her eyes she realised with a spurt of panic that it wasn't her mind playing tricks at all.

Because there he was.

Large as life.

In the same lift that she was about to step into!

He was in deep discussion with two other men. They moved in a tight group away from the lift and passed by the two women.

If Gabby had been quicker instead of being paralysed on the spot with surprise, she could have stepped behind Sally and hidden from his warm grey eyes. But she wasn't and she just gawped instead.

She held her breath as his eyes flicked towards her but he didn't appear to actually see her. Or simply didn't recognise her.

Thank goodness.

She let her breath out in a whoosh and the paralysis disappeared as quickly as it had come. Gabby hurriedly stepped into the lift, hoping Sally would follow without any delay.

The man's head suddenly whipped up. He spun around and stared. Hard. Straight at Gabby. His mouth opened as if to call out.

Grief, he had recognised her!

The lift doors mercifully closed on

his stunned face. Gabby was safe. She had made it. Just. Phew. She let out a long, heartfelt sigh.

'I agree with you,' said Sally, misinterpreting the sigh. 'He is one prize male. I would perjure my soul to have a date with him.' She made a low purring noise and rolled her eyes. 'I reckon he'd be hot.'

'Does he work here?' Gabby asked nervously. She hoped he didn't or she'd be on tenterhooks all the time. Please, please let him by just passing through the building on business.

'Oh yes,' said Sally with a laugh. 'I'd say he works here. All hours. More than anyone else, in fact. He's a shining example to us all.'

That was not what Gabby wanted to hear. The hairs on the back of her neck actually rose. She might bump into him at any given moment. Scary stuff!

But before she could ask anything more, Sally was taking her around to meet other members of staff who were in the canteen having coffee.

She tried to follow Sally's introductions but she wasn't terribly successful. Her concentration was shot to pieces. She was totally churned up and preoccupied after seeing That Man.

Who on earth was he? Was he a journalist too? She'd have to ask Sally, but tactfully. She didn't want her getting the wrong idea that Gabby was interested. Because Gabby wasn't. No way. At least, not much. But she needed to find out as much as she could about him so she could work out a plan of avoidance.

There was little opportunity to brood about The Man for the rest of the day as she was sent across the city to do a feature on what was being done for the homeless and didn't return until late.

* ★ *

For the next week she worked hard researching and writing her feature, which was due for the Saturday paper.

She saw little of Sally and nothing at all of The Man.

During the weekend, she slept in late, explored Perth and wondered what the following week would bring. She was nervous she might see the sexy stranger and she hoped she could maintain a cool distance that would end any misguided attraction between them.

The first thing to greet her when she returned to work was a memo on her desk telling her to see the news editor urgently. Uh-oh, Gabby was immediately worried that something wasn't right, that something had gone wrong with her feature.

'The story was great,' the news editor reassured her. 'But you're wanted upstairs.'

'Upstairs?' queried Gabby.

'The big boss himself wants to meet you after reading the homeless feature. He was impressed and wants to personally congratulate you.'

Gabby was given instructions how to get Sam Donovan's office. Within minutes she was standing outside his door with his secretary.

'He'll see you now,' said the woman and the next moment Gabby was in a huge office. It was splendidly furnished with native red Jarrah and modern art and had massive windows that gave magnificent views of the Swan River.

But it wasn't the décor and views that dried the introduction on Gabby's lips and stunned her into shocked silence. It was the man himself.

Sam Donovan.

Because he was That Man!

And he was regarding her in as much surprise as she was him.

'You!' he said. The warm surprise of his tone made Gabby's stomach flip and dip. She could feel her cheeks heating. She was acting like a gawky teenager. Again! She had to get a grip!

'Mr Donovan?'

'I'm so glad we have finally met. I was hoping against hope I'd see you again!' A genuine smile lit his face and he stood, holding out his hand to shake hers.

'Gabrielle Balfour,' said Gabby and she could have kicked herself for sounding so breathless. As if she'd run up the many flights of stairs to his penthouse office rather than taking the elevator.

'You're Ms Balfour?' He clasped her hand in his large, tanned hand. It was dry and warm and lean. Gabby glanced at their hands now intimately entwined. She swallowed a sudden constriction in her throat and swiftly raised her eyes to his. He was regarding her intently.

Too intently.

This was too much. She instinctively went into defensive mode.

'Mrs,' she quickly corrected. 'It's Mrs Balfour.'

She determinedly emphasised her married title. That should stop him in his tracks, she thought, trying to quell the crazy panic he inspired.

She was conscious of his eyes flicking to her left hand where she still wore her plain gold band.

'Married. What a shame,' said Sam.

And she could have sworn there was real regret underpinning his words.

Gabby forced a smile, 'It depends which way you look at it,' she said.

'Sorry, I'm being totally selfish. I was hoping we'd be able to get to know each other a little better.' His comment hung in the air, tantalising and dangerous.

'You made quite an impression on me the other day. I couldn't stop thinking about you.'

The flip and dip were doing their aerobics routine in her stomach again. Gabby tried to control the heat rising to her face. She must not blush again. She must not show that he affected her in any way at all, or that their feelings were mutual.

'As one of your employees, I don't think that would have been a terribly good idea. Do you?' she said and was appalled to hear the huskiness suddenly plaguing her voice, as if she were in the mid throes of laryngitis.

'It depends which way you look at it,'

he said with a self-deprecating smile as he echoed her words.

The man was too gorgeous for any woman's sanity. A lesser woman would have succumbed to his charms and admitted her widowhood, telling him she was free for whatever he had in mind! But Gabby blocked any intention of succumbing to temptation.

She couldn't be disloyal to Mark. All because Sam Donovan had a gorgeous face didn't mean she had to respond to him.

It would feel like cheating.

She still loved Mark. He might not be with her physically, but he was in her heart. That was all she needed.

Except Sam Donovan was making that same heart race dangerously fast.

3

'I'm looking at it my way,' declared Gabby, her voice still sounding sexily smoky much to her chagrin. 'And while I'm flattered by your interest, I'm not in a hurry to complicate my life.' She forced her lips into a smile to leaven her words. She didn't want to antagonise the man. After all, he was her new boss.

'Don't worry, Gabriella.' His expression softened as his eyes rested on her tight, nervous smile. 'I would never come between a man and his wife. And I would never compromise one of my staff.'

Well, that was a relief, thought Gabby, mollified.

'I'm glad to hear it,' she said, her smile now more spontaneous.

'But it doesn't mean I can't regret what might have been.'

Flip, dip. Dip and flip. That routine

was getting so old. The smile slipped and she tried to ignore her traitorous inner tumult.

'And,' he continued in the face of her sudden silence. 'It doesn't mean we can't be friends.'

'I don't even think that's a good idea,' she muttered half under her breath.

'But I'm being a little premature. Firstly, I'd like to welcome you on board The Western Standard. We're lucky to have a journalist of your excellent calibre.'

'You flatter me.'

'It's deserved. And I want to congratulate you on that homeless piece in Saturday's edition. It's the sort of investigative piece I'd like to see more of in the paper.'

'It was a challenging subject. I enjoyed doing it.'

'Good. I shall look forward to reading more of your articles. I do hope, Gabriella, that you'll be very happy working here.'

'I'm sure I shall if the first week was anything to go by.'

Sam's intercom buzzed and his secretary informed him he had another appointment.

'Thank you, Lee. I'll be free in a moment.' He turned towards Gabby. 'I'm sorry. I'd really like to carry on our discussion but I've pressing business to attend to. Maybe some other time.'

'Maybe.'

Gabby wasn't a bit sorry the interview was at an end. She was sweating buckets trying to maintain her cool composure. This man shook her. He threw her off balance with his easy charm and sexy voice and warm eyes and . . .

'Until next time.' Sam held out his hand to shake hers and end the interview.

Gabby stared at it. Did she really want to touch him again? But there was no choice without appearing rude. She gave his fingers a brief clasp with the tips of hers and then fled.

At home that night Gabby tossed a green salad and chatted to Mark. 'I reckon I should look for another job, what do you think, Mark? I don't want to keep running into Sam Donovan. He makes me very, very uncomfortable.'

Not that searching for another job thrilled her. It had been hard enough plucking up courage to go knocking on The Standard's door.

But thinking of Sam Donovan was pretty daunting too. He was causing all kinds of emotional havoc.

She placed the salad on the tiny white cast-iron table out on her tiny balcony and bustled back for her plate, already laid out with cold meat and potato salad, and her solitary wine glass.

She sat down and cast her eyes over the scene that was spanning out before her. It was early evening in the middle of the city and from her tiny rented townhouse she could see people heading out for their evening meal or to some sort of entertainment such as the theatre or one of the many wine bars.

The street lamps were replicas from a Victorian era and, in her opinion, were incongruous with the exotic backdrop of ornamental palms, giant tree ferns and purple and pink bougainvillea that hung in heavy profusion from balconies and balustrades.

The night was warm and clear and alive and Gabby felt privileged to be part of it. It was a long way from the damp winter cold of her dingy Brighton flat.

'But the thing is, Mark. I do like the other journalists on The Standard. They seem a nice crowd and I don't feel up to breaking any more new ground in the next few weeks. I don't want to do anything rash. I want to just settle down into a comfortable groove for a while and get my bearings. Is that so wrong?'

She waited a beat, as if he was answering her, and then said, 'No, I don't think so either.'

She munched on a celery stick and

cocked her head to one side. 'And I suppose, as Sam Donovan is the big boss and has assured me he doesn't mess with married women, I won't see much of him anyway, so I'm worrying unnecessarily.'

Actually, that thought depressed her as much as the idea of finding another journalist's position, but she resolutely didn't explore why.

'So I think I'll stay put. What do you reckon? Pretty sensible, love? Good. I'm glad you agree. I'll drink to our decision.' She clinked her glass against the bottle of red and took a sip. 'I'm so relieved that's sorted out. Bon appetite.'

★ ★ ★

Gabby didn't see Sam Donovan for the rest of the week, which should have been a good thing but, perversely, it was disappointing too. But she was making inroads with her job, forming friend-ships and getting the hang of her new environment.

'We're having a party,' Sally Essex announced to her that Friday.

'For anything special?' asked Gabby in a preoccupied fashion. She was proofreading her article before filing it away for the sub-editors to deal with.

And at the word of 'party' she had immediately shut down anyway. She had no intention of attending any parties in the foreseeable future. She hadn't been to one since Mark had died and she didn't feel like breaking that track record now. And besides, she would feel awkward going to a party on her own.

'Oh yes,' said Sally with bouncy confidence. 'It's a very special occasion. It's to officially welcome you to The Standard.'

Gabby's heart sank to her pink-painted toenails. Bother. There'd be no way of weaselling out of it then if it was in her honour. 'Where and when?' she asked and hoped she didn't sound too unenthusiastic.

'At the Eureka pub straight after work today.'

'I can hardly wait,' she said a touch glumly.

The Eureka was packed by the time Gabby had finished her shift and briefly smartened herself up for the ordeal to come. She elbowed her way through the crowd, greeting those she knew and being introduced to others, until she made it to the bar where Sally was already perched on a high barstool.

'Throw some dollars in the kitty and get yourself a drink,' said Sally with a grin. 'You've got some catching up to do, kiddo.'

The next hour or so whizzed by and Gabby had to admit she was actually enjoying herself. She couldn't remember the last time she'd been out with a crowd of friends. Perhaps she had been avoiding life for too long, because this was fun.

Or at least it was until Sam Donovan turned up and made it complicated.

The first she knew of his presence was when that warm, blue-metal voice growled a greeting only an inch away from her ear. Immediately all her senses were on red alert and her skin was goose-bumping.

She slopped her wine and actually squeaked in surprise. 'Grief, Mr Donovan, are you trying to give me a heart attack?'

'Sorry, but with all the racket in here, it was the only way to get your attention.' He grinned and raised his glass. 'Cheers! Welcome again to The Standard, Gabriella,' he said.

'Thank you, but what are you doing slumming it in this dive?'

He quirked a brow and his smile widened slightly, his eyes merrily crinkling at the corners. 'Well, of course I'm here because of you and the party. But I also own this, er, dive.'

'The Eureka?' Gabby felt her cheeks flame in embarrassment. Her and her big mouth! 'Sorry. I didn't know. No-one said.'

'No need to apologise. It is a dive. Which is why I bought it. I intend to refurbish it and make it one of the

41

classiest bars in the city. Perhaps you'd like to see the plans and give me your opinion?'

Gabby shook her head in knee-jerk reaction as panic flared within her. Surely that would be akin to agreeing to see someone's etchings, wouldn't it?

There was a slightly ironical gleam in Sam's eyes and Gabby felt her cheeks grow even hotter.

'What do you say, Gabriella?'

'Ah. Perhaps.'

'Which translates as 'no, not in this lifetime',' he said dryly, obviously reading her thoughts.

Gabby fleetingly raised her eyes to his and then dropped them again as she saw the unnerving warmth there. 'Well, it's awkward. You know . . . '

'Oh I know, Mrs Balfour. Believe me, I know.'

And what was she supposed to make of that cryptic comment? Best not to make anything out of it, but the implications were there. They hung between them, as did that crazy chemistry that seemed to pulsate whenever they met. Why was this happening, and now?

With Mark she had never felt this churning and burning inside. He had been more of a balm, a calming influence in her otherwise erratic life that had involved chasing news stories and delving into peoples' private lives with no set nine-to-five routine. With Mark, she'd known exactly where she stood. He'd been the one constant in her ever-changing world. And he'd been her best friend as well as her lover, which was why she missed him so much.

Sam Donovan was an entirely different story.

For starters, she didn't feel safe at all. He only had to speak and his rough-sexy voice reduced her insides to hot mush. When he regarded her with his dark grey eyes, a larva flow of something she didn't want to identify, flowed through her veins. And when he touched her she almost melted into a smouldering puddle on the floor.

It was crazy.

It was wrong.

It was downright scary!

Thankfully Sally chose at that moment to join them and the conversation ran on general, less dangerous lines for a few minutes. Then Sam spoilt it all by asking where Gabby was living.

'I'm temporarily renting a townhouse off Hay Street,' she said evasively. As Hay Street was a long street that went through several suburbs, she hoped she was safe divulging that much information. Not that she really expected Sam Donovan to make house calls. Not on married women or employees, at least.

'It's one of those nice ones down the Subiaco end,' offered Sally much to Gabby's instant dismay.

'If it's the ones I'm thinking of, they're tiny homes,' he said frowning.

'You've got it. It's dolls' house size,' responded Gabby.

'Those townhouses are barely big enough to swing a cat.'

'Good job I don't have one, then.'
Gabby allowed herself a glimmer of a
smile.

'It must be cramped for the two of
you.'

'Mark doesn't take up much room,'
said Gabby hurriedly, crossing her
fingers and surreptitiously kicking Sally's leg when the other woman's eyes
widened in surprise.

'That's lucky. What does he do for a
living? I don't think you've said.'

'He was a teacher back in England.
He, er, hasn't worked since we've been
in Australia,' she improvised and shot
another meaningful glance at Sally,
willing her not to give the game away.

'Get him to come and see me with
his references. I know someone who
can help find him a job.'

'That's very kind of you.' Gabby
could feel the prickle of perspiration.
She hated lying, but what was the
alternative? 'I'll tell him,' she said and
hoped Sam would end the conversation
there.

She was in luck. Sam glanced at his watch and said regretfully, 'I have to go. I've a theatre date.'

'That sounds nice.' she hoped she didn't sound too relieved that he was leaving and chatted on quickly to cover any rudeness. 'We used to go to the theatre a lot in England. Almost weekly.'

Sam raised one quizzical brow. 'If you and Mark are theatre buffs, Gabriella, I'll get you a couple of tickets.'

'I meant that I used to do reviews for the newspapers. I wasn't fishing for tickets,' she said, flustered her throw-away comment had backfired.

'I didn't say that you were. It would be my pleasure to get you tickets. A welcome-to-Australia gift for you and your husband.'

'Er, thanks.'

This was too awful. She would have to confess. But not now. She was too chicken. Too confused. And she didn't want an audience for her confessional. Just in case there was a scene.

As he left the bar, Sally turned accusing eyes on Gabby. 'So what was that all about?' she demanded.

'Which bit?'

'What do you mean, which bit? The bit where he thinks Mark is still alive, of course!'

'Well, yes. I suppose he does think that.'

'Suppose nothing. How come? Why haven't you told him the truth?'

'It's complicated, Sally. He knows I'm married but not widowed.'

'Why did you lie to him? What was the point?'

'I didn't mean to!'

'But you did. Saying that he didn't take up much room was a blatant, outright lie.'

'Well, yes and no.'

Sally rolled her eyes. 'For goodness sake. We're both journalists here. I know you're lying. You know you're lying. What's the deal?'

Gabby groaned. She'd often pumped people to get the truth for articles, but to be the one being grilled by an investigative reporter wasn't so pleasant.

'Come on, spit it out,' said Sally, resting her chin on her hand as if she was settling in for the long haul.

Gabby groaned again. 'Must I?'

'Yep.'

'All right, but it sounds daft saying it out loud.'

'I promise I won't laugh.' Sally crossed her heart and then cocked her head expectantly.

'Though Mark has gone physically, spiritually I still feel he's about, that he's with me.' She sighed. It sounded pathetic but it was the truth.

Sally squeezed her hand sympathetically. 'OK, I can see where you're coming from but why not come clean with Donovan? He's not someone to fool, you know. He ought to know the truth.'

'I know, but as I said, it's complicated.'

'I still don't understand why?'

Because he was interested in getting to know me better, Gabby wanted to shout. But she didn't feel it would be a good idea to fill Sally in on that detail.

'Let's just say it was for self preservation,' she hedged.

'Sorry, I still don't get it.'

Gabby shrugged. 'Believe me, it seemed the sensible thing to do at the time. But perhaps, in hindsight, it wasn't.'

Gabby nibbled her bottom lip. Because she knew full well it wasn't! She was in deep, deep trouble.

4

The theatre tickets were sitting on her desk Monday morning. Gabby gingerly picked them up. They were for the first night premiere of a Tom Stoppard play. She pursed her lips. Hmmm. She felt like a fraud. She'd got the tickets under false pretences. She felt bad. So now what should she do? Confess?

Her desk phone rang, interrupting her troubled thoughts.

'Gabrielle Balfour? It's Lee, Sam Donovan's secretary. Mr Donovan's out of town for a few days. He wanted to make sure you'd got the theatre tickets.'

'I did, thanks.'

'I hope you enjoy the show.'

'I'm sure I shall. Please pass on my thanks to Mr Donovan.'

Well, that took care of that, thought Gabby as she put the phone down. There was no way she could confess now. And it was probably best she didn't anyway.

He'd get used to seeing her around the place and lose interest in a while. She'd ride it out. No sweat.

★ ★ ★

'Did you enjoy the play?' Gravel and smoke poured down the phone receiver and swirled around Gabby as she sat at her computer terminal the day after the theatre.

'Mr Donovan!'

'Sam. Do please call me Sam. So did you?'

'How could I not,' she fought down the sudden breathlessness his voice invoked. 'They must have been the best seats in the house.'

A rich chuckle smouldered down the line. 'They were. They were mine.'

'Oh. I didn't realise. Thank you so much for letting me have them.'

'My pleasure. Did your husband enjoy the show?'

Gabby experienced a rush of blood to the head. Now was the time to confess everything but her tongue stuck to the roof of her mouth and her throat dried.

'Hello? Are you still there?'

She unstuck her tongue with an effort and cleared her throat. 'Er, he didn't go. He was, er, indisposed.'

It was lame but it was the truth. Well, sort of.

'I'm sorry to hear that. Better luck next time.'

'Yes. Look I have to go. Deadlines and all that,' she gabbled, her words falling over themselves in her haste to get away. No way did she want to prolong this conversation. It was fraught with danger. 'Thanks again.'

'You're welcome.'

Phew. She dropped the receiver in its cradle and rubbed her temples. Maybe she should put in her resignation now, before the going got too sticky.

But she didn't want to! She liked it here. She was being given interesting and challenging assignments and developing a high profile in the paper.

And if she left she wouldn't see him again . . .

She stared at the computer screen for a good long minute, not registering a single word. Then she resolutely shook herself.

She was being stupid. Of course, there was every possibility that he would lose interest and forget about her . . .

★ ★ ★

Sam replaced the receiver and pursed his lips thoughtfully. He was good at reading people and anyone would think Gabrielle Balfour had been in a hurry to get rid of him. Why? She had nothing to fear from him. He'd already told her he didn't hit on married women, but that hadn't seemed to allay her nerves.

So was there more to it than that? Was she attracted to him? He knew he was to her. Not that it changed anything. It wasn't in his make-up to date married women.

He'd personally experienced the fall out of divorce. His father had been woefully unfaithful to Sam's mother and the acrimonious divorce had destroyed the family. His mother had suffered a breakdown and Sam and his sister had been sent to boarding school. At thirteen, he'd vowed he would never knowingly be responsible for destroying a marriage.

And that vow still held good today, though for the first time ever he was sorely tempted. Gabriella had really burrowed under his skin.

But it wouldn't do.

Sam tried to push Gabriella to the back blocks of his mind and get on with the mountain of paperwork cluttering his desk. It didn't work. The pull of her exquisite face, with those hauntingly big, beautiful blue eyes that hinted at an inner sadness, kept hovering on the edge of his subconscious and prevented him from concentrating.

He found a flimsy excuse to enter the newsroom and he quickly cast his eyes about while discussing something totally trivial and unnecessary with the news editor.

He spotted Gabriella almost immediately. She was deep in conversation on the phone, the receiver propped between her chin and shoulder while she madly scribbled notes on a pad, asking questions, frowning and delving further.

Her auburn bob was dishevelled and he realised why as she dragged her fingers through her hair a couple of times while obviously querying something the other person had just said. She was dressed in a simple sleeveless shift that Sam would bet matched the colour of her eyes perfectly.

If only he could go over to her to see if he was right . . .

With only half his mind on what the news editor was saying, Sam continued to study Gabby. She closed her interview and began reading back over her notes. Someone called her name and she laughed at some comment they said.

There was none of the blushing shyness that she displayed with him. Instead she seemed confident and assured, a professional woman in total command of her destiny.

But then she caught sight of Sam and all that changed in a twinkling. Her pale skin flushed the colour of crushed raspberries and her cool poise slipped off-kilter so suddenly she was like a newborn colt — all limbs and no control.

She knocked over a tub of pencils and scattered papers on to the floor and then dragged her hand through her tousled hair, mussing it further.

Sam lost the thread of his discussion and smiled at her. Gabby nervously smiled back and then ducked her head so a curtain of auburn hid her face from his view. She began to collect up the pencils and papers, her movements jerky and uncoordinated.

Sam itched to go over to her and

brush the strands away so he could see her expression, but of course he couldn't do that. It would be professional and social suicide. But, goodness, he was tempted!

Stop! Remember who she was. That she was married. This was all madness, wanting her, needing her. He shouldn't even be here, succumbing to temptation. He had to get out of the newsroom, and now.

Sam abruptly terminated the conversation with the news editor and strode from the room, leaving the woman scratching her head and wondering what on earth Sam Donovan had been talking about for the past few minutes.

Back once again in his office, Sam paced up and down in front of the windows, but the tremendous views of the Swan River and Kings Park were wasted on him. All he could picture was that beautiful woman sitting at her desk several floors below him. She might as well be on the moon, he thought in frustration, because she was completely out of his reach and unobtainable.

He had to get things into perspective. Gabriella Balfour was married. He had to forget her for his own sanity's sake.

Which of course was easier said than done.

★ ★ ★

Over the next few days, he passed her in the corridors, in the lift, out in the street. She seemed to haunt him at every turn. And, although he didn't consciously seek her out, he found himself watching for her whenever the opportunity arose and then greedily drinking in the sight of her when he was lucky enough to strike gold.

But the more Sam saw of her, the more it occurred to him that Gabriella Balfour was one very sad woman under her bubbling personality.

The unhappiness hung over her like a hazy autumn mist. There was nothing tangible, just an aura of deep grief that cut Sam to the heart. He didn't want her to be unhappy.

But why was she so sad? What was going on in her life that quenched the vitality in those baby blues? That, when Gabby was in repose, gave her a defeated slump to her shoulders and shadowed her sweet smiles?

Sam wanted to know. But was he entitled to find out? After all, she was married. It was another man, a lucky man, who had that privilege.

Sam pondered about it for several days and then decided he had to do something, anything, to end his torment. He needed to know what was troubling Gabriella.

Perhaps her marriage was in difficulties? If he saw her interact with her husband, then he might have a better idea what was going on. It was a long shot, but Sam decided it was worth a try. He didn't question too deeply why he wanted to know the state of her marriage, but there was a glimmer of hope alive and hidden in his heart.

He once again had his secretary pass

on theatre tickets to Gabriella and this time he intended to be in the audience too and watching the Balfour couple carefully.

★ ★ ★

Sitting in a box opposite his usually reserved private theatre box, Sam waited impatiently for Gabby to appear. She was late and got there just before the lights went down. As she made herself comfortable, Sam narrowed his eyes and clenched his jaw determinedly. Because he wasn't terribly surprised that she had come alone.

So where was this mysterious husband of hers? Had they argued? Had he left her? Had they separated? The small glimmer glowed a little brighter, though Sam tried to ignore it.

He hated himself for wanting the Balfour marriage to be in trouble. Hated that Gabriella was hurting and that he wished he could be the one to comfort her.

In the bar during the interval, Sam looked in vain for Gabby. He ended up buying a bottle of wine, collecting two glasses and making his way to her box. He knocked on the door and walked in without waiting for an answer.

Gabby stared at him open mouthed. 'Mr Donovan!' she squeaked, her eyes wide open as if she'd been caught doing something wrong.

'All on your own, Gabriella?' he said smoothly.

'Well, yes.'

'Your husband couldn't make it again?'

'Er, no.'

'You haven't given me his references yet.'

'Um, I haven't.'

'Why not?'

'Erm, er, really there's no need.' She fluttered her hand in the air as if it didn't matter. 'I thought you were out of town.'

He allowed her to change the subject, just happy to be near her. 'I was. I came back early and didn't want to miss the show. It promised to be a good one. Do you mind if I stay here? I've come bearing gifts.'

'You're entitled to stay,' she said dryly. 'It's your box. These are your seats.'

'That doesn't mean I'll encroach if I'm not wanted.'

Gabby looked at him for the longest time as if she was having an internal battle with herself. Her expression was wary, but Sam didn't push her, didn't try to influence her, though it was hard not to.

He waited, reining in his urge to steamroller over her feelings and stay anyway, because that was all he desired.

'I'd enjoy the company,' she finally said, her voice quiet. Her long dark lashes swept down over her eyes so he couldn't read what was in those hyacinth depths. 'Please, stay.'

Sam felt a huge swell of warmth in his heart. Which was crazy but great all at the same time and totally out of proportion to her decision. It was like securing a fantastic business deal, or winning a pile on the horses, or being a kid again and finding Santa had left you a bulging stocking full of brightly-wrapped goodies.

'Thank you,' he said humbly, silently giving thanks. 'Would you like a glass of wine?'

Gabby nodded and Sam poured the rich liquid into the two wine glasses. He handed one to Gabby and then gently chinked the rim of his glass with hers in silent salute. They took the first sip, neither of them saying a word, just the air pulsing between them.

'So where is your husband?' He had to ask. He was unable to stop himself. He had to know. And was it his imagination or did panic flair in Gabriella's eyes?

'I'd rather we didn't discuss my private life,' she said, her voice trembling ever so slightly.

'OK.' There was another pulse beat of charged silence. 'So what shall we discuss, Mrs Balfour?'

'Something safe and non-controversial,' she said, twisting a strand of hair around her finger in a nervous gesture that wasn't lost on Sam. 'How about the play?'

He raised his brows slightly and gave a slight nod. 'The play it is, then,' he said.

5

It was midnight. It was hot. But Gabby was curled in a foetal huddle on her bed, clutching to her chest Mark's old chunky knit jumper which she hadn't washed since he'd died. She buried her nose into its scratchy folds and inhaled, trying to detect the scent of her husband, trying to hold on to something more tangible than a memory.

There were no surprises that her emotions were once again in turmoil. They always were if Sam Donovan came into her orbit.

She had thought things had settled down between them. She hadn't seen him, not really seen him, for a couple of weeks. She had hoped (well, she had, sort of) that he had lost interest in her.

But this evening had put paid to that theory.

Drinking ruby red wine in the close,

intimate confines of the theatre box had been an unnerving experience.

But enjoyable, said a traitorous inner voice that Gabby tried to ignore, but failed.

'What do you reckon, Mark?' she said into the semi-darkness. Her bedroom was illuminated by the outdoor street-lamps and glowed a muted orange while casting deep shadows into the corners. 'Do you think I'm playing with fire? Reckon I should get out while the going is good?'

Gabby strained in the silence to hear a message. Nothing was forthcoming. Just the benign hum of a city never asleep.

She sighed and stared unseeingly at the ceiling, thinking, remembering . . .

When Mark had known that he wasn't going to get better, he had told Gabby that he'd wanted her to find someone else and not to lock herself away in grief. She was too young to be on her own, he'd insisted. She wasn't cut out for the single life. She mustn't stagnate into widowhood but keep moving forward, being open to a new love. He'd made her promise that she would try and find somebody else.

And she had promised, but only to keep him happy. She hadn't meant it. At the time she couldn't contemplate ever falling in love again. She'd loved Mark and only Mark and the toll his death had taken on her heart had nearly crushed her. How could she envisage loving anyone else? Being open and vulnerable once again? The idea was frightening.

It was also totally ridiculous. No-one could replace Mark. But then the dark, forceful image of Sam Donovan rose determinedly before her. And suddenly it wasn't so ridiculous anymore.

She quickly thrust the thought away. No! It was still too soon. Much too soon. She still needed more time.

Her eyes rested on Mark's photo on her bedside table. Mark smiled back at her, vital and alive but locked in that glorious stormy day at Brighton Beach.

He was out of reach. Forever.

A tear slid down her cheek, rapidly followed by several more. The tears surprised her. Gabby had thought she'd been all cried out months ago. But something had shifted in her heart and even as she wept, she realised those tears were healing tears.

Perhaps she was finally moving on.

*   *   *

Gabby had the next day off. She slept in late, which was just as well considering her restless night tossing and turning and thumping her pillow. She took her time over breakfast and then later she ambled down to the shops and picked up milk, bread and a copy of The Standard.

Back at the townhouse, she made a coffee and settled down for a leisurely read of the newspaper. But before she'd read a single word, she was interrupted by the telephone. It was Sally.

'Have you seen the paper yet?' she

demanded without preamble.

'I've seen it but I haven't had a chance to read a single word yet,' said Gabby. 'And good morning to you, too.'

'Is it? Have a look at the social pages.'

Gabby flicked through until she came to the double spread of social pictures — smart, happy people grinning widely at the camera. She glanced at the headline. The function was the previous evening's opening night at the theatre. In fact the same performance she had attended.

Her heart skipped a beat. She rapidly scanned the photographs, knowing with a sinking heart what she was going to find.

And there it was. A big smiley picture of Sam Donovan, his head tilted cosily towards his companion. Which was, of course, her.

She'd vaguely remembered camera flashes going off all around her when in the foyer at the end of the play, but she hadn't even considered that anyone would bother taking her photograph.

She wasn't famous or a celebrity of anything remotely special.

But Sam was.

And because The Standard photographer had known both of them, he hadn't bothered approaching them for caption details and so hadn't been aware that they had been snapped.

Gabby groaned.

'Nice picture,' said Sally dryly. 'They're all talking about the merry widow in the newsroom this morning.'

'Oh no.' Gabby groaned again.

'Oh yes! You've caused quite a stir. Donovan isn't usually seen with us rank and file. I suppose he knows all about Mark now. How did he take it?'

'Actually, he doesn't know. I haven't told him yet.' Gabby closed her eyes in a pathetic attempt that all her troubles would go away, but they looked just as bad in the dark.

'Oh dear,' said Sally.

Oh dear was an understatement, thought Gabby in despair. 'I know, I know. I'm a complete fool. But the time hasn't been right.'

'I guess you know what you're doing,' said Sally, but the doubt in her voice was loud and clear.

'No. Not really,' Gabby had to admit. 'I'm just slowly feeling my way.'

'So the big question is, how long have you been dating him, you dark horse?'

'Good grief, I'm not dating him! I just bumped into him there. It was a coincidence.'

'Some coincidence. I wish he'd bump into me too sometime. He's the most gorgeous guy on the planet.'

'Feel free.'

'I wish. At least now I know why you're getting all the plum jobs.'

'What do you mean?' Gabby asked, surprised at the comment.

'Favouritism. You're the boss's pet.'

'Don't be ridiculous!'

'Gabby, apart from your first week, you've been getting all the top assignments and getting high profile in the paper with huge by-lines. It's making some of the long-term staff sick to their boots. Of course, I'm not one of them. You're a cracking journalist and deserve the exposure. It's just some of the others don't see it like that. Now you've appeared in the paper with Sam, they're bound to jump to conclusions.'

'I hadn't realised,' Gabby said, concerned. She had wondered at her luck in getting such a good run of jobs, but how galling to think it might all have been all Sam's doing. It took away the thrill and made her mad. He had no right to do such a thing, even if he was the boss . . .

'I must have a word with Dan Commeri. It can't be allowed to continue. I want to be treated the same as everyone else and be an accepted part of the team.' And she would have a few choice words to Sam as well, just in case he was pulling strings.

'Well, babe, you've certainly stirred up some feelings. And not just Donovan's. There's quite a lot of antagonism in some quarters.'

That was the last thing Gabby

wanted. She hated the dark side of professional jealousy. 'I'll talk to Dan next time I'm at the office,' she said. 'I'm so sorry, Sally. But you must believe me, there's nothing between Sam and I.' She crossed her fingers as she said that, just in case.

'OK. I believe you. Thousands wouldn't, of course, especially after looking at that photo. But don't worry about it.'

'I'll try not to,' said Gabby with a sigh. But she knew she would. How could she not?

'Look, I've gotta go. I only rang to warn you about the pic. I've got work up to my eyeballs.'

'I appreciate your call. Thanks, Sally.'

'Don't mention it. It'll probably all blow over anyway. Especially as you're not on roster for a couple of days.'

Gabby hoped that Sally was right but it didn't stop her worrying all morning. Should she ring Sam now and tell him to back off where her assignments were concerned? And should she tell him the truth about her marital status in case he heard about it through the grapevine? But would that be construed that she was actually open to a relationship when she wasn't? She didn't want to make things more awkward between them than they already were.

But then again, if he heard through somebody else he'd probably be angry that she hadn't been completely honest with him.

Tangled webs had nothing on it. She rued the day she'd ever bumped into Sam Donovan.

In the end Gabby decided to stop being a wimp and have things out with Sam. She rang Lee, his secretary, who then informed her that Sam was away on business for a few days.

The relief Gabby experienced was total. OK, so she was a coward, but at least she would have time to summon up a bucketful of courage before she next saw Sam and she had a feeling she would need all the courage she could muster.

* * *

When she fronted up to work a couple of days later she was greeted by the theatre critic, Felix Crowe. He was infamous for his biting wit and malicious streak. Gabby wasn't surprised that he was whistling the theme tune from the Merry Widow.

'Very funny,' she said as Felix perched on the corner of her desk and gave her a suggestive wink.

'Darling, you had us all fooled. We thought you were still in mourning for that mysterious husband of yours.'

'I am,' she said repressively.

'So how come you were dating the chief?'

'That wasn't a date. We simply met by accident.'

'But, darling, you were cosily drinking wine and watching the play from Donovan's private box. I wouldn't call that an accident.'

'That's where the usher took me when I presented my ticket,' Gabby

75

defended herself. 'Mr Donovan was sitting over the other side of the auditorium.'

He waggled his eyebrows. 'But I saw him sitting with you during the second half.'

'Only because we'd met up and decided to share the box. It was just a friendly arrangement between two colleagues, nothing more.'

'Colleagues? I wouldn't say you two were work mates, darling. More like the millionaire slumming it with the maid.'

'Mr Donovan is a professional and I am a professional so I figure we're equals,' said Gabby tautly. 'And anyway, Felix, I'd always been led to believe that Australia was an egalitarian society and completely classless. So again, I would argue that Sam Donovan and I are colleagues. Are you telling me I've got that wrong? That I'm missing something here?'

'There's class here like anywhere else,' said Felix with a smug smile. 'But it's based on position and wealth.

You've been rubbing shoulders with the elite, my sweet. What have you got the rest of us don't?'

Gabby could feel her temper rising. She shouldn't have to explain herself to this man. 'In your case, manners, perhaps?'

'Ouch, the cat's got claws.'

'Absolutely. Now go away. I've got loads of work to do.'

'But I haven't finished yet. When are you next seeing the big chief?' he pushed.

'That's none of your business!'

'I think it's very much of interest, though. I'm intending to do a little colour piece for the in-house magazine.'

That threw Gabby. Sally had said she'd upset people. Was this one of the ways they were getting back at her?

'No comment!' she said and tried to keep her face expressionless while she was seething inside. At that moment her phone rang. She snatched it up, glad for the excuse it gave her to ignore Felix.

Her respite was short lived.

'Gabby?' Smoke and gravel. Gravel and smoke. Gabby almost closed her eyes tight and waited. Why had Sam rung her now, with this parasite of a man sitting so close? It just wasn't fair. His timing was atrocious.

Then a horrible thought hit her smack between the eyes. Had he discovered she was a widow? Was he ringing to blast her? Though he didn't sound mad . . .

Gabby endeavoured to keep her voice neutral. She was endeavouring to do a lot of that this morning. 'Hello,' she said.

'Lee said you were trying to contact me.'

'Ah, yes.'

'Anything important?'

'Yes. I mean, no.' How could she discuss anything with Sam while Felix Crowe was breathing down her neck?

'Interesting.' He laughed. 'Well I have something I want to discuss with you. Are you free to come to my office?'

'Now?' Annoyingly it came out more of a panicked squeak than a calm question.

'As soon as you can would be good.'

Gabby's eyes flicked to the theatre critic who was straining to hear who was on the line. She turned her back. 'I'm due to attend a conference in a few minutes.'

'OK, don't worry about it then. I just wanted to tell you that I'm holding a party on Saturday night. I'd like you and your husband to come.'

'Where?' She tried not to sound rattled.

'My place.'

'But where's that?'

There was brief silence than a warm husky chuckle that danced along her nerve endings and shivered down her legs. 'You're probably the only person at The Standard who doesn't know.'

'I can tell you now, I'm not asking any of them!' she said tartly, excruciatingly aware that Felix Crowe was leaning closer and closer towards her.

79

Any minute now and he'd topple into her lap!

If she had to ask her colleagues directions to Sam Donovan's home she might as well wire a town crier to shout out that he wanted her to go to a party and see what everyone made of that! 'Please tell me.'

Sam gave her the address. Because Gabby still hadn't got the hang of all the street and suburb names, she had to jot it down on her notepad and hope against hope that Felix couldn't read her scribble.

The infuriating man smirked as she replaced the receiver. 'Well, well,' he said and slid off the corner of her desk and sauntered away, once again whistling the Merry Widow theme tune.

Gabby could have screamed.

When she returned from covering the conference it was late and most of the staff had left for the day. But Dan was still in his office and Gabby decided that it was a good time to tackle him about her assignments and find out if

Sam had indeed organised for her to have the best ones.

'Is it true?' she demanded a few minutes later.

'Yes,' said Dan bluntly. 'Not that you don't deserve to cover some of these stories,' he said. 'You're a damn fine journalist.'

'But I only got the breaks because of Sam Donovan,' she said bitterly.

'Yeah.'

'But why?'

'He liked your style.'

'My style? I don't understand.'

'You're the best person to answer that.'

There was no mistaking his meaning.

Gabby feel her cheeks flushing and her heart began to beat erratically. 'But there's nothing between us!'

Dan looked suitably sceptical, but said, 'Well, that's none of my business.'

'But it's true! There is nothing going on between Sam and me. Honest. Treat me like the other journalists. Don't cut me any slack or favours, regardless of whatever Sam Donovan has decreed. Please. I demand it!'

'No can do. What about Donovan?'

'To hell with Donovan. He doesn't own me.'

'No, but he owns the paper and what he says goes. Take it up with him if you've got a problem.'

The interview at an unsatisfactory end, Gabby didn't know if she'd achieved anything except the dubious fact of bringing out into the open this strange relationship between herself and Sam Donovan.

She marched back to her desk, determined to have the issue out with Sam when she saw him, and started to organise her notes from the conference. At least that was something she could do with confidence.

She worked until late and then went home and fell into bed, absolutely exhausted. But however tired she was, she couldn't help but stress about her strange relationship with Sam, the trouble she was in with her work colleagues and worry about the article Felix Crowe was going to publish in the in-house magazine.

'Mark,' she said in the orange-tinted darkness. 'My life is a mess. Could it get any worse? I do wish you were here . . . '

6

'I want you to cover an exhibition opening at the State Art Gallery,' Gabby was informed by the news editor the following day. 'You don't mind working a Friday night?'

'Not at all,' said Gabby. 'I've no plans for the evening.' Except another lonely meal on her balcony and an early night with a book. She was more than happy to forgo the evening's entertainment.

At six-thirty she made it to the gallery where she was given a glass of champagne and a glossy catalogue of the exhibits. There was already a crush of people there, most of who seemed to know each other.

Like the opening nights she had attended at the theatre, it was the city's well-heeled smart people laughing and drinking and catching up on the gossip of a world alien to Gabby.

She moved away from the crowd and began studying the paintings on show. They were by a West Australian artist of whom Gabby had never heard and were an eclectic mix of modern and traditional.

She wandered about, making notes about some of the pieces and eavesdropping the patrons' conversations. Red dots were being rapidly placed alongside some of the paintings as people made their choices and Gabby mused on which ones she would have bought if she'd had the money.

She didn't know what made her look up, but suddenly she felt breathless and tight-chested. She glanced towards the gallery entrance and there was Sam Donovan looking dark and strong and vital and splendid in a dinner jacket.

His dark hair was slicked back and damp. His hair had grown longer since they'd first met and Gabby liked the way a lock suddenly fell forward on to his tanned forehead. He swept it back as he turned to his companion and

Gabby's chest constricted some more, this time with a sharp emotion she didn't want to identify, but it was remarkably akin to jealousy.

His companion was a woman and she was stunning. She was tall and blonde and slim and could easily have been a supermodel.

Sam dipped his head towards her, though only slightly because she was almost as tall as him, and he laced an arm around her narrow waist, pulling her with him through the crowd. They made their way towards the artist who was standing in the middle of a chattering group of well-wishers.

Gabby spun away as she caught the warm smile Sam gave the unknown woman. It was like the special smiles he gave her. He had charm, and of course he would use it on other women, Gabby didn't have a monopoly on it. But for some perverse reason, it rankled just the same.

Her senses hummed like a tuning fork as she retraced her steps through the exhibition, trying to get as far away from Sam as possible.

Her excuse was that she didn't want to chance another encounter with a photographer and end up splashed over the social pages of the newspaper again. She was having difficulty living the last one down and there was still that worry of the so-called colour piece appearing in the company magazine.

But in reality, Gabby didn't want to see Sam. And she didn't want to meet his lady. And she didn't want to go through the pretence of politeness. She didn't feel she could cope.

Suddenly the whole evening had lost its allure. She no longer wanted to absorb the atmosphere and revel in the artistic beauty surrounding her. She wanted to go home to her solitary meal, her book and her bed and hug Mark's dark blue jersey close to her chest to bring her comfort and make her feel less alone.

But she couldn't leave yet. She had her job to do. She half-heartedly jotted down more notes about some of the pictures. She leaned forward to get a closer look at a stylised still life study when, buzzzz! The electronic security system went off.

Gabby reared back as if burnt and a guard gave her a hard, suspicious look. She shrugged sheepishly and mouthed a sorry. Then the same thing happened again when she inspected another picture. This time the buzzer sounded much louder, though that could just have been her guilty imagination working overtime.

When it happened a third time, Gabby sighed in resignation. When she'd hit puberty she'd gone through a stage of generating too much static electricity.

She'd been unable to wear a wristwatch because the hands speeded up too much and if she'd been too close to the radio it had crackled. The phenomenon had stopped once she had met and married Mark.

Obviously it was now reasserting itself. What a great way to announce its arrival. It was probably because she was so wired up with all the trouble in her life.

She sighed again when two hulking security guards came bearing down on her. This was really making the evening one to remember.

'I didn't do anything,' she protested as they towered either side of her. She had the distinct impression that they were going to frog-march her ignominiously out of the exhibition as if she was a two-bit criminal. Brilliant. All she needed now was The Standard's photographer to capture it on film and it would be the cherry on the top of the cake.

'Truly, I didn't do anything,' she said.

'It's OK, Nick, she's with me,' said a smoky-gravel voice right behind her. 'I can vouch for her.'

Did she detect a quiver of laughter under that gravel and smoke?

Make that a dozen cherries on top of the cake! Gabby wished she could curl up and die.

'I didn't do anything,' she said again. 'I was just looking closer at the picture.

Like this.' She leaned over the red-corded rope designed to keep the public at arm's length and the buzzer went off on cue.

'You must be pumping a heap of electricity around that sweet frame of yours,' said Sam with an even more pronounced quiver.

'I can't help it,' she muttered. 'It happens sometimes.'

'I think it's cute,' he said and then took her hand, which made her jump as if she had been on the receiving end of an electrical jolt.

Gabby tried to tug her hand away. She was still mad at him for organising her assignments. But now wasn't the time to yell at him about it. They were surrounded by people.

Sam just smiled and held on tighter. 'I'm glad you're here,' he said. 'There's someone I want you to meet.'

The next moment she was shaking hands with the tall blonde. 'This is my sister, Rachel. She's staying with me for a few weeks before returning to

Sydney,' he said and Gabby would have been lying to say that she was suddenly inordinately pleased that this woman was his sister and not his lover.

Which was crazy. And stupid. Because she was not interested in Sam Donovan! She was cross with him and fed up for being tagged his favourite by her colleagues. And she wanted to dump him and run.

Oh, who was she fooling? She was interested. Big time. And she was more than curious to meet his sister.

'So nice to meet you,' said Rachel whose voice was low and sweet. She was as lovely close up as from afar and Gabby couldn't help but envy Rachel's graceful curves and poise. She was pure model material.

Being barely over five foot, Gabby had never achieved the elegance that seemed as normal as breathing to tall women. She suddenly felt like a gauche, squat dwarf at a fairy convention.

But Rachel's smile was friendly and she soon put Gabby at ease. After a few polite pleasantries, Rachel said, 'Have you met the artist yet, Gabriella?'

'No, there was too much of a crush. I've been having a good look at his pictures instead and getting a feel for his style.'

'Well, do come and meet him now. He's an old friend of Sam's and he's absolutely fascinating.'

The artist, Luke Sommers, was as tall and fair and graceful as Rachel. He wore a black silk shirt in a gothic style that exposed far too much oiled, bare chest for Gabby's taste.

His eyes were a feline-yellow — lazy and watchful. He was lapping up the attention like a well-fed cat but his gaze became more acute as the Donovans and Gabby approached.

'Ah, at last,' he said. He held up his hands towards them, index fingers to thumbs, as if to frame a picture. 'Exquisite,' he murmured with rapture. 'Totally exquisite.' The other people standing around him dropped back and turned to see what or whom he was referring to.

Gabby glanced towards Rachel, presuming that she was the subject of Sommers' admiration. It was a shock when Luke Sommers suddenly reached forward and took a strand of Gabby's hair between his long, paint-stained fingers and teased it between the pads of his finger and thumb.

'Oh!' Gabby's head kicked back and cracked against Sam's chest. His arm instinctively wrapped around her waist and held her close.

For a magical moment there was a complete feeling of peace and security. Something precious that Gabby hadn't experienced for the longest time. How she wished it could go on for eternity . . .

'Don't shy away,' said Luke, his fair eyebrows lifting imperiously. 'Your hair begs to be touched. It's smooth and silky like gossamer.'

'Don't be ridiculous!' she said, embarrassed both by his words and gesture but even more so by Sam's intimate embrace.

But Luke wasn't listening to her protest. 'I must paint you,' he enthused, then intoned low and dramatically, 'Why so pale and wan, fond lover? Prithee, why so pale?' . . . '

'Pardon?' said Gabby, feeling even more flustered. She wasn't the sort of girl people usually quoted poetry over. This was crazy.

'I saw you earlier. You looked so sad, little one. I was hoping we could meet. I must capture that subtle sadness on canvas. It begs to be heard. 'Better by far you forget and smile than that you should remember and be sad'.'

He stroked her fringe away from her brow and cocked his head on one side, frowning slightly. 'Is it grief that makes you mourn? Or perhaps lost or unrequited love?'

'Please, don't!' Panic suddenly swelled in her chest as her grief rose to suffocate her. It felt as if a balloon was lodged in her breastbone and was being pumped full of helium to bursting point. What was this man doing? Trying to expose her raw inner pain?

Sam's arm tightened further as if he could feel her meteoric rise in tension. His embrace was meant to comfort her but Gabby felt trapped. How could she escape if Luke Sommers stripped bare her soul?

She stared wide-eyed at Luke, willing him to go no further. He smiled slightly. 'I'll plump for the lost love.'

He raised his golden eyes to Sam. 'I shall call it Frozen Maiden. Or Fire and Frost. What do you think, Sam?'

'I'll commission you, mate,' was Sam's blunt response. 'But only if you promise to keep your hands off her. I know your reputation too well, you rogue.'

'It's all true,' sighed Luke theatrically. 'The women simply aren't safe around me. They find my artistic temperament irresistible.'

Sam gave a short laugh. 'I would have said it was totally resistible. But I mean it, Luke. You might be my friend, but I don't want you giving Gabriella any trouble.'

'So that's how the land lies,' Luke said, his heavy lids hiding the gleam of interest in their watchful depths.

'If you want that commission, you bide by the rules,' Sam grinned back, not disclaiming anything.

Gabby gawped like a stranded cod before finding her voice. 'You two can't be serious? I don't want to be painted!'

Rachel giggled. 'Don't be so coy. I would love to have my portrait done,' she said. 'Would you paint me too, Luke?'

The artist flicked a look in Rachel's direction and then back to Gabby. 'Only if this adorable young thing will sit for me.'

'How about we discuss this over dinner?' said Sam.

'I won't change my mind,' declared Gabby. 'I will not be painted.'

Sam smiled down into her eyes. 'Let's have dinner anyway.'

No, no, no. That wouldn't solve anything. She'd just fall deeper into the mire.

But she couldn't help but respond to his warm smile. As her lips curved and her brain tried to formulate a good excuse to turn down dinner, there was a sudden flash.

Her smile died and Gabby briefly closed her eyes. She knew what that flash meant. They'd been caught by The Standard's social photographer again.

Reluctantly opening her eyes, she saw the photographer grinning all over his face and looking very pleased with himself.

'Evening, Mr Donovan,' said the man. 'Evening Mrs Balfour.'

'Oh grief,' said Gabby as the photographer moved away to snap other unsuspecting victims.

'What's the problem?' inquired Sam, securing a couple of glasses of champagne for them while Rachel monopolised Luke Sommers' attention.

'We're going to be in the paper again,' groaned Gabby.

'Is that a bad thing?'

'Awful.'

Sam chuckled. 'You don't seem very keen about being immortalised in print or paint, Mrs Balfour. But let me set your mind at rest. Luke's an old friend of mine. He won't try anything on. He's also a damn fine artist. His work is becoming very collectible.'

'Listen carefully, Mr Donovan, I — don't — want — my — portrait — painted!' Gabby enunciated slowly.

'But it would be wonderful to capture your quintessential beauty on canvas. How could you deprive future generations of that experience?'

'For goodness sake, stop it,' said Gabby feeling very hot and flustered by his sudden intensity. If she went near any of the exhibits now, they would all buzz at once she was feeling so hyped up and nervous. 'It's really embarrassing you saying things like that. I'm no pin-up. I'm completely ordinary. And I don't want my painting done.'

'I disagree with you. You're special . . . '

Gabby held up an imperative hand to

silence him: 'And it would be a complete waste of time and effort, not to say money, because no one in their right mind would buy the painting anyway.'

'I would.'

'You're obviously not in your right mind,' she said loftily.

'That's true.'

'See!' But she felt a mite miffed that he admitted it so promptly. He could at least keep up the pretence rather than shoot down her ego!

A slightly crooked smile tugged at Sam's lips and Gabby could have sworn his expression softened.

'Because,' he said softly so that the hairs at the nape of her neck rippled at his sudden tenderness. 'Since meeting you, Mrs Gabriella Balfour, I've had a very hard time thinking straight.'

'Oh,' she said inadequately.

'I know I'm out of order saying that, but I can't help it. You fill all my waking moments and invade my dreams. Your husband is one hell of a lucky bloke. I envy him from the bottom of my heart. I hope he appreciates and cherishes the treasure he has in his possession.'

Gabby's eyes involuntarily filled with tears. She loved and missed Mark. And she was more than a little confused about her feelings for Sam. His silence, tender words weren't helping either.

'I'm sorry,' he said huskily, half raising his hand to brush the teardrop trembling on her lashes but then dropping his arm as he remembered where they were. 'I shouldn't have said that.'

She wordlessly shook her head.

'Gabriella, it's none of my business the state of your marriage, but I do get the feeling something isn't quite right between you and Mark. If there is anything I can do . . . '

'Actually,' and her voice was as husky as his. 'There is something. I really must tell you.'

'Ah.' He sipped his drink and regarded her quizzically over the rim of his glass. 'Is this what you wanted to talk to me about a few days ago?'

'One of the things.'

'I'm intrigued. Go on.'

She felt too vulnerable to discuss Mark, but she could tackle him about the assignments. Anger was an easier emotion to handle. She squared her shoulders and launched her attack. Sam heard her out in silence.

'Is it true?' she said.

He shrugged. 'I only wanted you to have the best.'

'But you can't single me out for that sort of attention. It makes my position untenable. You have to understand that.'

'But I like to help my friends, Gabriella.'

'I do appreciate where you're coming from, Sam, and I am grateful. But look at it from my point of view. The relationship with my workmates is important. I don't want it jeopardised by being given the top jobs before I've earned them. Please don't interfere again or I'll have to resign.'

She held his eyes boldly, not backing down.

'I see.'

'Deal?'

'You're a hard woman.'

'Shake on it.'

Sam held her hand. His was warm and strong and she could feel her pulse kick up. She let go quickly, but Sam continued to hold hers. 'So what else did you want to discuss? Mark?'

Gabby nodded slightly and ducked her head. She stared at the bubbles rising and popping in her frosted flute. This was one of the hardest things she'd done for a long time.

She didn't want to discuss Mark's death and her deception. The gallery was too public a place. Saying that, confessing in private didn't hold any allures either.

'Gabriella? Talk to me. Share with me. I might be able to help.'

'I don't think now is the right time,' she hedged. 'It's better said in private.'

'Over dinner?'

'No, not over dinner.'

He stared at her for a long moment, trying to gauge what was going on. 'OK,' he finally said. 'What about tomorrow night? You could tell me then.'

'Tomorrow night?'

'At my party.'

'Ah.'

'You will come?' There was an edge to his voice that disturbed and thrilled Gabby. It sounded as if he really, really wanted her to be there.

Rachel interrupted them before Gabby replied. 'Sam, there are some people I want you to meet.'

'I'll be with you presently.'

'Now, darling. They are about to leave.'

'All right.' He held Gabby's eyes with his. 'Gabriella . . . ?'

'You'd better go. And yes, I'll see you tomorrow night.'

As soon as Sam left, Gabby put her half empty glass on a tray and fled the gallery before anything else embarrassing could befall her.

7

'You like her,' said Rachel at breakfast the following day. She was studying the social pages in the weekend paper. A big photograph took centre stage of Sam gazing with blatant intensity at Gabby.

'Who?' said Sam, sipping his coffee. He was deep into a financial report and barely listening.

'Gabriella Balfour.'

At Gabby's name he raised his eyes and met those of his sister across the breakfast table. She grinned as she handed him over the newspaper. He glanced at the photograph and then gave back the paper.

'Yes, I do,' he said simply and resumed his reading, though he was very aware of his sister's continued scrutiny.

'So?'

Sam sighed and put down his report. 'So, nothing. She's married. There's no future in it.'

Rachel continued to stare at him. 'I wonder if that's the attraction,' she said.

'What?' This time he didn't raise his head but re-read the same paragraph for the fourth time.

'That it's safe for you to fall in love because there's no chance of having to make a commitment.'

'Playing the amateur psychologist, Rach?' But he acknowledged the hit. Before he'd met Gabriella, he'd been happy to only date women where there was no danger of a long-term commitment.

But now he felt differently. He wanted more than just an affair.

'I don't waste time on hypothesis.'

'But what if she were free?' she insisted. 'Would you have an affair with her then?' She sipped her coffee and waited for his answer.

Sam threw down the report on the table and rose to his feet. 'No,' he said and saw the disappointment wash over her face.

He smiled a touch wryly. 'No, I'd marry her,' he said and had the satisfaction of his sister choking on her coffee at his surprise admission.

The taxi dropped Gabby outside of the floodlit waterside mansion where the party was already in full swing. She very nearly turned tail and clambered back into the back seat, but the driver wasn't wasting any time. He was already swinging the car around to head off down the wide driveway and back to the city. She was stranded. The only way was forward and into the lion's den.

Squaring her shoulders and readjusting her plain black shift for the six millionth time since she'd put it on, she headed towards the open front door.

A waiter in a white tuxedo ushered her towards the ballroom and offered her pink champagne in a frosted flute. Gabby stood there on the threshold, clutching her glass, and feeling frozen and alone even though the night air was hot and sultry.

There must have been three hundred people chatting in the magnificent marble and glass room, and she felt totally and miserably out of place.

What on earth was she doing here? Suddenly she had a lot of sympathy for Cinderella. How had she felt turning up at the palace ball in a pumpkin-on-wheels and magic glad-rags with no social graces? But at least she'd had a fairy godmother to back her up and a Prince Charming to rescue her.

Gabby had no-one.

She sipped the champagne while her eyes sought Sam. There he was, with a jovial crowd of men and women, laughing at someone's joke. And then his eyes met hers and the chilled mouthful of champagne exploded in her mouth so that bubbles went up her nose and caused her eyes to smart.

Sam extricated himself from the group and came immediately to her side. 'I'm so glad you've come,' he said missing her cheek and drawing her forward into the melee. 'You're alone? Your husband's indisposed again?'

Did she detect a certain irony in his question? She chose to ignore it. 'That's what I have to talk to you about,' she said instead, aware her voice was tight and strained. 'Can we go somewhere private?'

'Now? But of course. Come this way.'

But before they had moved very far, they were interrupted.

'Ah, the Frozen Maiden of my dreams,' drawled a voice. 'Darling, you should be wearing red or purple, not that hideous black. It hides your fire. Do come and dance with me so I can exercise my considerable charms and persuade you to pose for a portrait.'

Gabby didn't have a chance to decline. Luke Sommers tucked his arm around her waist and whisked her on to the dance floor. She was still clutching her champagne glass and trying her hardest not to spill its contents over the other dancers.

She looked helplessly towards Sam and his eyes were burning with the same intensity she'd seen the previous night. The same intensity the photographer had captured in his photograph in the morning paper. The same intensity that would be the subject of yet more gossip in the newsroom.

'This is crazy,' she said to Luke. 'I don't want to dance.'

'The only crazy thing I know of is not meeting you earlier. You're divine.'

'And you've drunk too much champagne. Let me go.'

'Not until I've got you far, far away from Sam. He's far too possessive. I don't want him snatching you away from me before I've had a chance to get to know you better.'

He danced her through the massive french doors that led out on to a terrace festooned with fairy lights and tried to kiss her in the shadows of a jacaranda tree.

'Oh no you don't!' she said, arching away.

'But darling, we're made for each other. When are you going to let me paint you?'

'Never.'

'Too cruel. You can't say that.'

'I just did. Now if you can't change your tune, I'm leaving.'

'Cold heart.'

'Practical.'

'I'm slain.'

'You'll live.'

'Who is killing who here,' demanded that beautiful, sexy gravel and smoke voice that immediately made Gabby's heart beat faster.

'Sam!' She had felt nothing while being held in the arms of Luke or listening to his outrageous compliments, but Sam's voice sent her pulses hammering.

'Your heartless Merry Widow is killing me softly,' said Luke rolling his eyes and clutching his heart as if he was in the throes of death.

Gabby's own heart screeched to a halt at the mention of the Merry Widow and then began pounding for all it was worth. She shot a glance at Sam. He was smiling slightly.

'Why Merry Widow?' he said. 'Have you suddenly killed off your husband, Mrs Balfour?'

'I . . . er . . . ' Gabby floundered, not quite knowing how to answer.

'Because she is a merry widow,' said Luke quaffing more champagne, oblivious of the sudden tension.

Sam looked from Gabby to Luke and then back to Gabby as the import of Luke's words sunk in.

There was an imperceptible tightening of Sam's mouth as his warm smile disappeared. There was an ominous narrowing of his dark eyes.

'Oh, didn't you know, Sam? Well, I am surprised. I thought everyone knew. Felix Crowe told me last night that our gorgeous creature here has been widowed for more than a year. All the men are desperate to woo her.'

Gabby opened and shut her mouth but nothing came out. Not even a squeak.

The silence crackled between them. There was suddenly an ear-splitting explosion.

A burst of light and a thousand fireworks began cracking and pluming in the sky as the evening's entertainment began.

But the spectacular show was wasted on at least two of the partygoers. The bright lights starkly lit their features and Gabby could see the storm gathering in Sam's face. Anger throbbed out of him in ever growing waves.

He looked ready to explode like one of the shockingly bright firecrackers overhead. She had to get away. This was terrible. She'd never seen someone so furious before. And it was all focussed at her.

But before his wrath erupted, a white-coated waiter approached Sam. 'Mr Donovan,' he said. 'You're needed urgently on the telephone.'

'It can wait!' His voice was harsh. More gravel, less smoke and it shook Gabby to the core with its bleak ferocity.

'I'm sorry, sir. Your sister said it was vital you took the call.'

'I'm on my way.' He spun around to Gabby. 'Stay here. Don't leave. I think you have some serious explaining to do.'

He stalked off into the house, his back taut, his shoulders braced for action and his head high.

'Oh dear,' said Luke, tut-tutting. 'I don't think Sam's very happy.'

Gabby all but slumped in a heap. 'Understatement. Thanks for telling him,' she said to Luke not attempting to keep the bitterness from her tone.

'But why, darling? Was it a big secret?'

'No. Of course not. But Sam didn't know.' She felt like bursting into tears, but really she only had herself to blame. She should have told him the truth from the start.

'How come? Why hadn't you told him if everybody else knows?'

'It's complicated.'

'Like?'

'I didn't want Sam thinking I was

available. I still love my husband.' She didn't add that she was also in danger of falling in love with Sam, because even she hadn't come to terms with that little gem yet.

'Oh dear,' said Luke.

'I feel awful.'

'Perhaps you'd better leave.'

'That,' said Gabby with feeling. 'Is the most sensible thing you've said tonight!'

She didn't waste time but disappeared back into the ballroom and made her way around the dancers to the main hall, feeling even more like Cinderella, except it wasn't close to midnight. But in spite of Gabby's haste, she wasn't quick enough. As she approached the open doorway, Sam appeared from nowhere and grabbed her arm just above the elbow.

'Oh no you don't,' he said through clenched teeth. 'We have unfinished business.'

'Sam!' She tugged, trying to loosen his grip.

'This way,' he said unrelentingly,

oblivious to the scene they were causing. He led her into a panelled study which was lit only by a green retro desk lamp. It cast little light but long shadows and Gabby could smell leather and polish and a hint of cigar smoke. It was a very masculine room. On another occasion, Gabby would have been entranced by it but now she shivered nervously, intimidated.

Sam locked the door behind them and then turned, leaned back against the solid jarrah door and crossed his arms. He looked mad. His jaw was set, his mouth was a thin, ugly line and his eyes were hard and brittle.

Gabby found it difficult to swallow and her body was shaking. 'Is locking us in really necessary?' she said, panic sharpening her words.

'I want no interruptions. Is it true? Are you a widow? Is your husband dead?'

She raised her chin in a self-defensive gesture. 'Yes. He died almost eighteen months ago.'

'Why the hell didn't you tell me? You led me to believe you were married!'

'I was. I am!' She held up her hand, the wedding ring glinting dully in the dim light.

'You played me for a fool!' He dragged his hand agitatedly through his long black hair and gazed at the ceiling as if seeking guidance. Suddenly he pushed away from the door and jerkily strode towards her, placing his hands on her shoulder and glowering down at her.

'I didn't play you for anything, Sam Donovan. When I told you that I was Mrs Balfour, I wasn't lying. It's the truth. That's my name.'

She twisted away from his grip and moved behind a studded leather arm-chair, using it as a physical buffer. 'But I do admit,' she added quietly. 'That I wanted my marital status as a safety barrier between us.'

'Why, for goodness sake? It makes no sense,' he growled. 'I was attracted to you. I wanted a relationship with you. I

116

wasn't going to hurt you.'

'Perhaps not. But I wasn't taking any chances.'

'So you lied and put me through hell.' His bitterness sliced deep.

'Not intentionally,' she cried. 'I thought you'd get bored with me and move on. I was told a little of your reputation when I first arrived. You were used to dating beautiful socialites. I didn't think you would waste too much time on me.'

'No, Gabriella, I was foolish enough to fall for you, in spite of thinking you had a husband. After my parents divorced, I always vowed I wouldn't touch a married woman but there I was, bowled over by one Mrs Balfour and despising myself to the core of my being.'

'The only thing that kept me sane was the fact your husband was never around. I thought you were having marital problems and hoped that if ever you were free, there would be a chance for me. But the irony was, you were free all the time. How you must have laughed.'

Gabby helplessly shook her head from side to side. 'I tried to tell you.'

'Not very hard.'

'It was difficult, Sam. But I'm sorry. I didn't mean to hurt you.'

'I'm not hurt!' he denied, though he was, deep, deep down. 'I'm damn frustrated and furious and feel mad that you've put me through hell. I've wanted you, Gabriella. Needed you!' He refrained from admitting that she'd filled his dreams and gate-crashed his heart. 'And now I discover that all that suffering was unnecessary. I could have had you any damn time I pleased.'

Gabby wrapped her arms around herself in an age-old defensive gesture as her own anger awakened. 'No, you couldn't have,' she said with quiet, frozen dignity. 'I wouldn't have let you.'

'You couldn't have stopped me,' he said cruelly. 'The attraction was mutual. If I'd turned on the heat you would have melted in my arms, Mrs Balfour!'

'I wouldn't have!' she protested angrily. 'I have more integrity than that.'

'Don't over estimate yourself. You're a passionate, hot-blooded woman. You couldn't have stopped yourself.'

His damning words had a ring of truth, which made Gabby even wilder.

'Believe me, Donovan, you're totally resistible.'

He snorted in disbelief. 'Would you like me to prove to you just how resistible you find me?'

'No!'

They glared at each other. The silence pounded between them.

'Tell me why you lied!' He couldn't hide the raw anguish that whipped out and joined his anger.

It struck a chord in Gabby and she flinched, but she still held her ground. 'I didn't lie. I told you, I still considered myself married. I wasn't looking for personal complications. I had enough to contend with learning to live without Mark and starting life in a new country.

But suddenly there you were, obviously interested and I panicked. You made be feel flustered and nervous. I didn't want that. I didn't want to feel so much. I'd had more emotion to contend with. I didn't want any more.'

'But the attraction was immediate between us. You admit that!'

'Yes, but I didn't want to get involved with you or any other man. Mark hadn't been gone that long. I still loved him. Still do.'

'But you could have told me!'

'What! I don't think so. 'Hello Mr Donovan, by the way I'm newly widowed and fancy you rotten!'' She shoved her hands on her hips and glared a challenge at him.

'Do me a favour, Sam, we'd only just met. I didn't know a damn thing about you and I'm not the sort of person to bare my soul in public.'

'You still should have told me. I would have understood.'

'Oh, so it's my fault?' she snapped back. 'You wouldn't have considered me being rather presumptuous? Rather forward by telling you I was available?'

She'd scored a hit. She knew that by the way he recoiled.

'OK,' he said ramming his clenched fists into his trouser pockets and hunching his shoulders like a schoolboy found out in a misdemeanour. 'So I might have questioned your motives, but I would have listened. At least I wouldn't have gone through this hell.'

'Well, I'm sorry if I didn't consider your feelings, Sam Donovan. I was too busy protecting my own. The trouble is you're so used to getting your own way, you don't stop to consider other people. I heard you were tough in business but I think that relates to your private life too.'

'When things don't run smoothly, you get mad. Well, I'm sorry to disappoint you, Sam, but married, widowed or just plain single, I wouldn't consider a relationship with such a man!'

'And this is your final word?' His face

had become a stark mark, his dark grey eyes glittering with black fury.

'Yes. And I'll inform you now, to avoid any further embarrassment, that I shall hand in my notice. Now unlock that door. I want to go home and I never want to see you again.'

8

Gabby spent Sunday manically cleaning her house from top to bottom and washing every item of clothing in sight. She spent the day alone and simmering. She didn't even enter into her usual dialogue with Mark because it gave her no comfort.

Actually, she did try once but it was as if he had gone into hiding and didn't want to listen to her rant and rave, which made her even madder. What was it with the men in her life? Were they in conspiracy to cause her maximum pain?

And why had Mark chosen now, of all times, to disappear on her and withdraw his support? Was he telling her that she was on her own now? That she had moved beyond needing his comfort and support? That she had reached the stage to fly solo?

Well, if that was the case, his timing was lousy. As was everything else in her life at the moment.

On Monday morning she was back at her desk, scratchy eyed and headachy from lack of sleep and tanked up on caffeine to get her through the next few hours.

She gave Dan Commeri her resignation mid-morning. 'You can't do this!' he protested. 'Why are you going? What will Donovan say?'

'It's because of Sam I'm leaving,' she said. 'Though I'd appreciate it if you kept that reason quiet.'

'He won't like it,' said Dan.

'He's expecting it,' she said.

'Oh. I see.'

'No you don't, Dan. Don't even try to understand what's going on. But believe me, Sam Donovan will be glad to see the back of me.'

But Gabby was wrong and Dan was right. Sam didn't like it when Dan personally handed him Gabby's letter later that day.

'I refuse to accept it,' said Sam, briefly reading through her letter and then scrunching it up and tossing it in the bin. 'Tell her to come and see me if she's got a problem with my decision.'

Half-an-hour later Gabby steamed into his office with another copy of her resignation. His gut immediately clenched at the sight of her. She looked gorgeous in her blue shift dress and shiny auburn hair, red spots of anger cresting her cheekbones and giving colour to her usually pale skin.

'You have to accept it,' she said, the fire of battle in her eyes. 'And if you throw this one away, I'll simply give you another.'

'And I won't accept that one either,' he said brusquely.

'Then I'll just leave anyway.'

'And I'll sue you for breach of contract.'

'I hate you, Sam Donovan!' she said and swept back out of his office, her small back rigid, her head held high.

Sam watched her go. She really got

under his guard. He was still angry at her prolonged deception, but however mad he was with her he didn't want her to march out of his life and never come back.

He threw his pen down on to the pile of papers that were awaiting his signature on his desk. This was crazy. They couldn't go on like this. The anger was like a canker in his soul, eating him alive from the inside out. It was affecting everything he did.

He would go and see her tonight. Damn, no. Not tonight. He had yet another endless meeting to attend. And he had meetings all the following day, so it would have to be the evening.

Perhaps something could be salvaged from this crazy situation.

* * *

'You can't leave!' declared Sally when she heard of Gabby's resignation.

'Watch me.'

'But why?'

'It has nothing to do with Sam,' she snapped.

'And as for you, you're as brittle as glass.'

'It's the weather. The heat is getting to me.'

'We're in air conditioning.'

'And the hot nights mean I can't sleep properly so I'm irritable.'

Sally rolled her eyes. 'Tell me what's really going on?'

'Nothing. I've just decided it's time to move on.'

'Let's go out for a drink tonight and you can tell me all about it.'

'Sorry. I'm working.'

'Again? You've worked every night this week. You're meant to be a part-timer and you're doing more hours than the regulars.'

'So?' said Gabby. She had volunteered for everything going with the reasoning that anything was better than sitting in her tiny townhouse and wondering why her life was in such a mess. 'It keeps me occupied.'

'That's sad.'

'That's life.'

'Well, if you're so intent on working until you drop, you can swap with me. I'm rostered to go away on a three-day fact-finding mission down south but it's my mum and dad's anniversary while I'm away.'

'Say no more. I'd be happy to escape the city for a few days.'

And escape the brooding presence of Sam Donovan.

And the ominous disappearance of Mark's comforting one.

★ ★ ★

At the empty townhouse, the telephone kept ringing. Sam slammed his receiver down for the thousandth time. Where was the woman? He prowled around his study. He desperately wanted to talk to Gabby, apologise for his atrocious behaviour the night of the party and ask her to give their relationship another chance.

He didn't want her to resign from the paper. He didn't want her walking out of his life.

He wanted her. Needed her. He would beg on bended knees if necessary. He'd do anything to have her in his arms and close to his heart.

He tried the phone number again and it rang out once more. He decided to go to her house and try and remonstrate with her, tell her that they did have a chance of love. That he'd be prepared to wait until she was ready.

That was, of course, if she'd have him.

Within minutes Sam was in his Mercedes and roaring over to the Hay Street complex. He rang the bell and knocked on the door. There was no answer.

Now he was really worried. Had she left and gone back to her home in England? He would follow her to the ends of the earth if only he knew where she was.

'Are you after Gabby?' said the

woman from the next-door house. 'She hasn't been around for a few days. I think she must be away or something.'

So she had gone.

Sam felt sick to the pit of his stomach but he wouldn't be beaten. He wouldn't let her go without a fight.

* * *

Sam was finding it hard to concentrate. He was involved in some high-powered discussions over a new business venture that needed his full concentration if he was to pull it off, but Gabriella Balfour was dominating his mind.

It hadn't helped that a copy of the in-house magazine had landed on his desk and he'd read the story about the attractive new merry widow on staff. There was a sketchy history of Gabriella's former newspaper positions and then it detailed their night at the theatre.

There were innuendos and not so subtle references about her relationship with him. His fists clenched as he held the paper. He'd like to string up Felix Crowe for trivialising and cheapening something so special.

Sam then transferred his attention to the big glossy photograph accompanying the story. It was of him and Gabriella standing close together in deep conversation, oblivious to the other theatregoers surrounding them. He remembered how good it had been just talking with her and sharing the evening. She had been excellent company, warm and funny and sweet.

Sam's gut twisted. He'd so enjoyed that night. He wished they could start again. Go back to before harsh words had been said. He needed to speak to her . . .

But where the hell had she gone? He considered hiring a private detective to track her down but then dismissed it. He would find her himself, but first he had to tie up this contract and delegate his other work.

9

When the first news reports hit of the bushfire, Sam took a cursory interest. It wasn't close to Perth and so was of no immediate danger. As for the news coverage, he had complete faith that his reporting team would do a good job without his interference.

By evening the fire was raging out of control. Homes were being evacuated. The fire fighters were having a hard time due to the high summer temperatures and strong easterly winds that were fanning the fire and making it burn across bush and farmland at a horrifyingly fast rate.

Sam had a business function that night and didn't catch up with any further information about the fire until the following morning over breakfast. And it was Rachel who alerted him to the trouble.

'Hello, grumpy,' she said when he came in from a long swim and sat down to have his breakfast. 'Feeling in a better mood this morning?'

'There's nothing wrong with my mood.'

'Sweetie, you've been impossible,' announced Rachel. 'I don't know what's getting to you, but really you should try and be a bit nicer to people. You've upset your housekeeper, the gardener and your secretary and they're the ones I know about. I dread to think how you've been treating your employees at The Standard.'

'If they don't like it, they can leave.'

'You must be in a state.'

'Shut up, Rachel, or go back to Sydney. Now, if you've finished with the paper, I'd like to have a quick read before I go to the office.'

Rachel grinned, unfazed by his grouchiness. 'I haven't but you can have the business section.' She perused the front page and then whistled through her teeth, 'Your friend is in the thick of it,' she said. 'Must be scary and exciting at the same time.'

'What are you going on about?' said Sam, barely listening.

'Gabriella Balfour. She's The Standard's correspondent for the fires.'

The next moment the coffee pot went flying. Rachel squealed a protest as Sam snatched the paper from her grasp and read the by-line with his own eyes.

He swore and threw the paper down so it landed in the spilt coffee. No wonder he hadn't seen Gabriella the past few days. And he thought she'd left. Instead she was in the thick of one of the worst bushfires in Western Australia's history.

In his study, he punched in the number of The Standard and demanded the company's mobile phone number on which he could contact Gabriella. He rang the number. A synthesised voice told him politely that the phone was out of range. Sam swore again and hit re-dial. The same voice repeated the impersonal message.

'Why the hell did you let her cover the fire?' demanded Sam as he stalked into Dan Commeri's office half an hour later. 'She's totally inexperienced where bushfires are concerned. You should have sent someone more savvy with the situation.'

'She was already on the spot. It was the sensible thing to do,' Dan protested. 'Anyway, Sam, Gabby is a professional. Let her get on with it.'

'Send someone else to relieve her. She must get out of there fast. They're saying it's totally out of control. Gabriella could get hurt. Killed even.'

Dan gave him a level stare. 'We don't play favourites at The Standard Remember?'

'This is different. This is Gabriella!'

'Gabby has always insisted that she be treated like the other staff. You know that. I know that. She was mad when you interfered before.'

'This is different. I don't care what

135

she wants in this instance. You get her out. Now!'

'I'm sorry, Sam. No can do. We've already sent another team, but Gabby and Brent, the photographer, will stay in position. I want them to continue to cover it. I'm not taking either of them off the job.'

'You didn't hear me, Dan. Get her out of there.'

'I'm the editor. It's my call.'

'I'm the boss. You get her out!'

'No.'

The flat negative ignited Sam's short fuse. The anger that had been eating away at him all week now found a dangerous new direction. He blasted Dan for putting Gabriella in danger, he railed at the fool who had purposely lit the fire and he swore at the weather.

Dan listened in stony silence until Sam had finished his tirade and had stormed out of the office. Dan knew the man was upset, but there was nothing he could do about it. He hadn't been game to tell him that he'd already asked

Gabby to back off and she'd refused to, point blank.

'I'm a professional, Dan. This is my job. It's what I do. Don't ask me to compromise myself just so you and Sam Donovan feel a little easier.'

'But the boss won't like it,' he'd said.

'He can lump it. I'm not standing down while my colleagues are thrown into the thick of it. I couldn't live with myself. I'm part of a team. Let me be a key player.'

So Dan had let her stay. If Sam wanted her out of harm's way, he'd have to go and do the knight-errant stuff himself.

Sam blazed a trail to his penthouse office where he prowled up and down in ever increasing frustration, listening to reports on the radio and watching live TV coverage. He'd read and re-read Gabby's front page eye-witness account until he knew it off-by-heart and back-to-front. His blood ran cold at the thought of her being in the epicentre of such a huge natural disaster.

If anything happened to her, he'd never forgive himself. He knew it was his fault she'd wanted to escape the city. She had wanted to get away from him and his boorish behaviour. It still made him embarrassed how badly he had acted.

Usually he prided himself on his manners and total control, but he had lost it big time. Gabby had been right. He was used to getting his own way and he didn't like it when thwarted. And because of it, his dear, sweet girl was now in danger.

The latest news flash came on the TV. Fire fighters from around the country were being flown in to help combat the blaze that was devastating thousands and thousands of hectares of bush and pastoral land. The prime minister had declared a state of emergency and had ordered troops to be made ready. The Red Cross was already asking for donations.

Sam felt impotent. Everyone seemed to be doing something except him. But what could he do?

Firstly, more importantly, he had to know if Gabriella was safe. She'd filed a report that morning but Sam hadn't personally heard from her. She hadn't answered any of the messages he'd left on her mobile phone message bank. He didn't know if that was because she didn't want to speak to him or if she wasn't able to. The not knowing was driving him mad.

'I'm going to the scene of the fire,' he told his secretary. 'Order the company helicopter.'

'It's already at the fire, Mr Donovan,' she said. 'It took the second news team to the scene.'

'Then charter me a private one.'

Two hours later, Sam was in the air with the disturbing, frightening news from Dan Commeri that Gabby was missing. She'd gone with one of the fire fighters and radio contact had been lost.

★　★　★

Gabby was scared. Nothing had prepared her for the nightmare of a wildfire. The sky was burned an orange hue with black and grey billowing smoke. The acrid stench of charred flesh of burnt animals was in the air along with the pungent, bitter smell of burning eucalyptus.

It was what she'd imagined a war zone to be like. It was as if she was locked in some surreal sci-fi movie, but instead it was terrifyingly real.

The hills and valleys and massive sweeps of paddocks were steaming black-scapes where the fire had already wreaked its havoc. Trees stood like skeletons, others had been felled by the flames. A section of fencing was destroyed. The posts were like rotted teeth in a wide-gaping giant's mouth and its wire was burned to pathetic whispers. It would never again prevent stock from roaming.

There had been so much damage in so little time, which made it more horrifying. She'd seen pictures of Hiroshima. This was similar. Destruction was swift and sure and extreme.

Gabby shuddered. She was exhausted. The heat didn't help, or the relentless wind that maliciously fanned the fire, spurning it to greater wicked mischief.

She took a swig from her water bottle. The water was as warm as blood, but at least it moistened the back of her raw, dry throat. She wiped the back of her wrist over her perspiration-wet forehead, pushing away her damp, lank fringe. What she wouldn't do for a long, cool shower and icy drink.

'Hey, Gabby, we'd better get back to the checkpoint,' said Craig, the fire fighter who'd volunteered to show her some of the worst hit spots. She'd been recording the scenes on a spare digital camera she'd been given by the photographer.

'Good idea. I've seen enough to last me a lifetime.' She jumped into his battered utility truck with its hot, cracked vinyl seats and dusty dashboard. The ute was kitted out with a fire-fighting unit on the back and the water sloshed back and forth in the tank as they headed along the road.

'The wind has changed direction,' said Craig, peering through the bug-splattered and smoke-grimed windscreen.

'Really? I hadn't noticed.' Gabby looked tiredly out of her side window. It had been a long couple of days and she was exhausted to the bone. She was wanting to get out of here, away from the heat and stench of burning carcasses and into fragrant fresh air, perhaps by the ocean, and then sleep for a week. 'Is that good or bad?'

'Hopefully it'll swing the fire back towards the burned out places. It should make it more controllable.'

'Let's hope,' she said and closed her eyes for a few moments' respite.

The fire did swing back, but more quickly than expected. Gabby and the fire fighter were still several kilometres from the checkpoint when they got into trouble. Within minutes the road was thick with black, billowing smoke and they couldn't see a foot in front of the vehicle.

'If anything happens,' said Craig calmly,

winding up the window and indicating that she should do the same. 'Stay in the ute until the fire has gone over. There're a couple of wool blankets in the back. Put one of them over you. It'll help keep off the worst of the radiant heat. Once the fire passes over, we'll get out and try and put out the spot fires.'

Try? Was there any doubt they wouldn't put the spot fires out? Gabby nervously bit on her bottom lip.

Craig noted her anxiousness and smiled at her.

'We'll be OK,' he said reassuringly. 'Don't you fret, love. Mind, it's a good job we kitted you out in protective gear.'

Gabby wordlessly nodded her head. She'd balked at wearing the orange fire retardant suit and boots when she'd first fronted up to cover the fire, but the fire fighters had given her little choice.

It was kit up or get out. Now she was thankful she'd listened to them. She wouldn't have fancied being out in the fire in her cotton slacks and open-toed sandals.

Nevertheless, Craig's words didn't give her that much comfort. She could see the concern deeply etched in his face. It probably mirrored her own.

Oh my goodness, she thought, we could be for it.

In a rush, she thought of Mark. Though she missed him like crazy, she didn't know if she was ready to join him with the angels any time soon.

She wanted to live! There was still so much she wanted to do.

And then immediately she thought of Sam.

Yes! Sam.

She wanted to have the chance to salvage her relationship with him. It pierced her to the soul that there was so much bad feelings between them and that it was all her fault for holding on to the past and not embracing the future when the chance had arisen to love again.

The past week had been awful, what with the anger and coldness mounting up between her and Sam like a summer storm, ready to break at any moment.

She wished she could say sorry and have the chance to try again.

And she so, so wished she could tell him that she loved him.

'OK, girlie,' said Craig, interrupting her troubled thoughts. 'If I drive any farther blinded by this smoke, I might hit something we're likely to regret. Sit tight. We'll be fine.'

He killed the engine and they sat there, listening to the dreaded roar of the approaching fire.

★ ★ ★

They dragged the blankets from the backseat and got ready to huddle under them when the fire hit. And hit it did, with an astounding, angry ferocity.

It howled around them, on them and over them for what seemed an agonising age. It screamed like a jet engine, constant and enormous.

The wind whipped the vehicle, rocking it backwards and forwards with its dreadful, unrequited wrath.

Gabby could hardly breathe with the suffocating, intense heat and smoke. It scorched her lungs and made her skin blister and burn, but at least the woollen blanket helped insulate her from the worst of it.

'Right, that's it. Out we go,' said her companion after what seemed an age. 'Careful you don't burn yourself on the door handle.'

They fought the fires with stalwart desperation. When the tank ran dry, they continued to beat the ground around them as sparks re-ignited with the gusting wind.

'I reckon it's safe to move on now,' Craig said after a while and they drove, this time without incident, back to the checkpoint.

★ ★ ★

They passed a farm. Only a couple of buildings were left standing, smouldering and forlorn.

There were the remains of trees that

were now black sticks with not a single leaf left on them.

Gabby was so weary she almost fell out of the ute when she opened the vehicle door. She was black from head to toe. She was scratched, burnt and singed but so very glad to be out of the fire front.

'We better get the two of you to the hospital,' said one of the police officers. As he led Gabby and Craig towards a waiting ambulance, Gabby suddenly heard a familiar voice.

She snapped upright. Sam? But it couldn't be. They were a good two, three hundred kilometres from Perth.

But then she saw him. He looked totally out of place in his charcoal grey business suit and startling white shirt among the soiled scruffiness of the volunteers and orange-suited emergency crews. But saying that, she noticed his tie was off and the shirt unbuttoned. And there was an intense, rumpled desperation about him.

He was gesticulating wildly and

determinedly at one of the police officers. 'But you must have some idea where she is,' he was yelling. 'You can't just lose someone. Tell me where she was last heard of and I'll drive there myself!'

'We can't let you do that, mate,' said the officer with ill-concealed patience. 'I know you're concerned, but our first consideration is your safety. We have to keep members of the general public out of the fire area.'

'I don't care about the risk,' shouted Sam, running his hand through his hair so it peaked untidily, trying to intimidate the officers with his bluster. 'I'm prepared to take full responsibility for my actions.'

'Not good enough, I'm afraid, mate. If we have to come after you, it'll be putting my men in danger.'

'I must find her! She could be lying hurt . . . '

'I'm sorry, but you must stay here. I'll let you know as soon as we have radio contact. Now if you would please stand to one side?'

'Sam?' Gabby said, but her voice was so smoke damaged only a bare croak emerged.

'Miss, let's get you in the ambulance,' said the young policeman.

'But,' she croaked again, though it painfully hurt her swollen throat. 'I think that man in a suit is looking for me.'

10

'Excuse me, sir,' said the young police officer, interrupting Sam's angry tirade. 'But there's a lady who wants to see you.'

Sam swung around and looked in the direction the man pointed. A small blackened figure in ill-fitting orange overalls was staring back at him. She half lifted her arm in acknowledgement and the next moment he was running towards her, eating up the ground between them with his long strides.

He wrapped his strong arms around her, pulling her into a rough embrace. 'My God, I thought I'd lost you,' he said thickly. He then slightly moved back and slowly, slowly he reached out and touched a strand of her hair. It was no longer smooth and silky but matted, sweaty and singed.

Black streaked her face and a purple

bruise peeked out from her fringe. She reeked of smoke and the soured scent of sweat and fear.

But to Sam, Gabriella Balfour had never appeared so beautiful and precious.

'I was terrified I had lost you,' he said and his fingers now moved to the delicate sweep of her soot-smudged jaw. He then cupped her head and drew her close again, holding her against his heart and giving a silent prayer of thanks.

He felt her hands creeping up his chest, clutching his shirt, scrunching the material tight in her fists as if she'd been thrown a lifeline, and he hugged her closer.

'I thought I was going to die,' she said, her throat working against the damage the smoke had wrought. She buried her face into his solid body and she began to cry.

He hugged her tighter, wrapping his arms around her slight frame and rocking her back and forth like a child, and just stopped himself from saying that he'd thought she was going to die, too.

'You're safe now.' He too was finding it difficult to speak. Raw emotion clogged his throat, making it hard to form words. 'I won't let anything happen to you,' he said thickly.

'Excuse me,' interrupted the same young officer. 'The ambulance is waiting. We have to get the lady to hospital.'

'I'm not letting her out of my sight. I'm coming too,' said Sam and led her to the waiting medics.

★ ★ ★

Gabby was curled up on her couch. The french doors were open and the evening breeze wafted in over the balcony. It was late, but she couldn't sleep. She'd spent all day in bed, sleeping away the horrors of the fire, and now she felt wide-awake and restless.

As usual, the city was buzzing. It

throbbed and hummed like a swarming bees' nest. Gabby nursed her cup of tea and was glad of the noisy activity. It made her feel less alone.

Of course, she didn't have to be alone. It had been her choice. After Sam had flown her back to the city in his personal helicopter, he had invited her to stay at his place. Had insisted. But Gabby hadn't felt right about it. There were things they needed to discuss and sort out before they could renew any sort of relationship.

So she'd asked to be taken straight home and after that, Sam had become silent and withdrawn. Gabby had felt too exhausted and confused to explain her reasons.

When her doorbell suddenly pealed, it made Gabby jump, slopping some of the cooling tea. Gabby glanced at the clock. It had gone midnight. Sam was the only person she could think of who would call on her at this time of night. Her heartbeat skittered faster.

'Who is it?' she asked in her

smoke-damaged, husky voice into the intercom.

'It's me. Sam.'

Gabby took a deep breath to settle her quickening pulse rate as she buzzed him in. He was wearing black tuxedo trousers and white shirt. The jacket and bow tie had been discarded. The top two buttons of his dress shirt were undone so that crisp dark chest hair peeked from the V-opening. Though his face was drawn, etched with deep lines of fatigue and anxiety, he was still gorgeously sexy.

His dark eyes swept over her and he smiled. It was a tentative but tender smile and lightened the deeper worry lines. Gabby could feel a blush tingle in her cheeks.

'You look gorgeous,' he murmured and drew a finger gently down the contour of her cheek.

Gabby was suddenly conscious of her under-dressed state. She was wearing one of Mark's old T-shirts that skimmed to her mid-thigh. It had been washed so many times that the material was soft and thin and moulded itself to where ever it touched. She should have remembered and taken time to throw on her wrap. Her blush began to rush and roar.

'I, er, better put something on.'

'Not on my account. I love the casual look.' His grin widened. 'I was coming back from a charity function and saw your lights on. I wanted to see how you were and,' he raised his brows ruefully, 'I thought you might like some company.' He tucked a stray curl behind her ear.

Gabby tugged down the hem of the T-shirt and felt her cheeks burn redder.

'I've been dozing all day and now I can't sleep,' she said, feeling suddenly gauche and awkward. She slid into the gallery kitchen to hide behind the breakfast bar. 'Do you want a drink of something?' she said and began filling the kettle anyway to try and dispel the heated tension surfing the tiny room.

'Do you have any whisky?'

'No. Sorry. Just wine.'

He shook his head. 'Nothing for me then.'

But Gabby had to do something. She prepared herself another herbal tea, though she didn't really want it. At least it kept her hands busy and an excuse not to look at him.

'How are you feeling?' he asked after watching her fumble the mug and spoon in the tense silence.

'Better, though my throat and chest are still sore from the smoke. The doctor said it would take a while.'

'A bit like heartbreak?'

There was a pulsating pause and Gabby ceased her jerky actions. 'Ah,' she said. 'That takes longer, but you do recover.'

'So I'm told.'

'Time is the only healer.' She said it more to herself than to Sam, but his lips quirked slightly in acknowledgement.

Gabby swallowed and didn't trust herself to speak. There was a sudden lump in her throat that hadn't been caused by smoke inhalation, but by the love she'd felt in the past and was feeling now.

'And how far are you healed, Gabriella?'

Gabby shyly raised her head. Her eyes were now filled with unshed tears that made Sam's handsome face shatter into tiny pieces as if she was looking through a kaleidoscope. 'I'm not sure, but I think I'm almost there,' she whispered, barely audibly.

'Really?' he whispered back.

'I think so . . . '

'I hope so, from the bottom of my heart.'

'Oh Sam . . . '

'Hush, my love. It's been a difficult time for the both of us.'

'I didn't mean to cause you any heartbreak.'

'I know, sweetheart, I know. But for a while there I was terribly angry. You'd blasted into my life and turned it on its head. I questioned that why, with all the cities in the world, you chose to come to mine and then proceed to destroy me.'

He grimaced. 'But you were right, you know, I wasn't used to being crossed in business or in love. It's been a very humbling experience loving you, Gabriella Balfour.'

'I'm sorry.'

'Don't be. I deserved it. I know you still love and mourn for your husband, but it's breaking my heart. I love you so much too.' Gabby tried to smile, but it came out a little lop-sided. 'That's good to know,' she said, her voice trembling.

'It is?'

'You asked me why I came here? Well, actually, you have Mark to thank for that. He wanted me to come.' She hesitated for a moment and then took a deep breath. 'Before he died he urged me to follow our dream. My dream. Which was to come to Australia. So I did and suddenly there you where. And it was all too much and I panicked.'

11

Sam stepped into the small kitchen and gently laid a hand on each of her shoulders. 'Gabriella?'

She allowed him to draw her close so she could feel the warmth of his chest through the thin white material of his shirt and feel the thump, thump, thump of his heart. He leaned his cheek against her hair and murmured, 'You don't smell of smoke anymore.'

'I used lots of shampoo.'

'You smell of strawberries and lazy summer days.'

'And you smell of Irish coffee and summer nights.'

'So do we complement each other?'

'Maybe . . . Yes.'

Sam gently led her to the couch and nestled her in to the crook of his arm. 'Tell me about Mark. Help me to understand.'

So, while Sam rhythmically stroked Gabby's arm, she told him about her husband, their life together and then his illness. Tears trickled down her face as she said, 'For a long time I felt his spirit was close and I took comfort from that. When I told you he was with me, I truly felt he was. I didn't intentionally lie.'

'So I've been fighting a ghost?'

'There was no fight. There is no contest between you and Mark, Sam.'

Sam stilled. 'Are you telling me there's no chance for me? For us? I love you, Gabriella. Don't my feelings count for anything?'

'Of course they do. But you have to understand that I do still love Mark.'

'I know,' his voice was suddenly bleak. He slumped his shoulders forward and dropped his head in his hands. 'Luke Sommers told me as much on the night of the party.'

'Yes, but what Luke probably didn't tell you was that I love you too,' she whispered, her heart pounding hard at her confession. The words hung heavy in the air and Sam lifted his head slowly. He gazed at her intensely.

'Do you really mean that?'

'I do. It's true. I love you.' She smiled, her lips trembling slightly. 'Since knowing you, I've felt Mark's presence less and less. It was as if he knew that it was the right time for us to set each other free, but it was still difficult for me to let go completely. It felt too soon, too final. I'd lost him once and I wasn't ready to lose him a second time.'

'But then you and I had that row and everything was so tense between us and I turned to Mark. But I found that he'd gone and that made me even more wild. I felt the men in my life were ganging up against me.'

'And then I realised that I was to blame. That it was all my fault. I'd orchestrated the whole awful affair. If I'd been upfront about being a widow we could have been happy from the word go. Instead I made us both terribly miserable.'

She sniffed and wiped her brimming

161

eyes with the back of her hand. 'Then there was the fire and I was stranded in all that black smoke and flames and I thought I was going to die. And the worst thing about it wasn't dying, but not being able to tell you that I loved you.'

She sniffed again. 'I'm so sorry, Sam. Can you ever forgive me?'

'Forgive you? Never! And do you know why, my precious girl?' He hugged her so close she was in danger of having her ribs cracked.

'Tell me.'

'Because there is nothing to forgive.' He nuzzled his lips into her hair and murmured, 'We love each other. That's more than enough for me.'

He then pulled her on to his lap and gazed into her tear-bright eyes. 'And, Mrs Balfour,' he said huskily. 'Do you think you're ready to wear another man's ring? Will you marry me?'

'Yes, I'll marry you, Sam. I'd be more than proud to call myself Mrs Donovan . . . '